TIME TRAVELLERS OF DWARKA

Story of Revati, the princess who Time-travelled

Inspired from a story of Mahabharat and Devi Bhagvatam

Bibhuti Shankar Das

books

Published By

Redgrab Books Pvt. Ltd.

942, Mutthiganj, Prayagraj, 211003
www.redgrabbooks.com
contact@redgrabbooks.com

Price in india : 250/-

Paperback, First published by Redgrab Books in 2024
Copyright © 2024 Bibhuti Shankar Das

Printed and bound in India
Cover Design & Typesetting by Redgrab Books team

ISBN : 978-93-95697-74-3

Author's Note

Sanatan Dharma, as the name suggests, is the eternal dharma. It is a way of living enriched with all the learning and experiences that has been gathered by humankind in the course of survival, and bestowed upon the humanity by the divine. Its richness is evident from its scriptures. The Vedas and Puranas contain the concepts and stories that show how technologically advanced and culturally rich our past has been.

The story mentioned in this book is an amalgamation of a historical story as narrated in our *Itihaas* Mahabharat and in a Devi Bhagavatam Purana, and a fictitious story from the author's imagination.

That part of this story which contains religious characters is not fictitious, rather is from Hindu religious history. Whereas the part which contains modern day characters is purely fictitious. This mix of modern-day characters with the religious story has been done to make the Puranic story and teachings more relevant to the present-day situation.

This work of fiction is a tribute to Shri Krishna and the lessons he has taught to humankind that are still showing us path of righteousness and will always be a source of strength to humankind.

My Krishna...
You are my strength
and you are my pride
Your words guide me
And makes me take stride

Hey Narayan...
I bow before you
Seek your blessings
and your love
to make beautiful musings

Oh Keshav...
Give me the strength
to perform my karma
and determination
to follow my dharma

Bibhuti Shankar Das

PROLOGUE

Time repeats itself. It is this cyclic nature of time that causes the change of Yugas – from Satya Yuga to Treta Yuga to Dwapar Yuga to Kali Yuga and then Pralay. Seventy-one such cycles make up one *Manvantar*. At the end of Manvantar comes the Maha-Pralay. Maha-Pralay is the total destruction.

What was created and flourished has to be destroyed. Destruction is inevitable, and that paves the path for the next creation. After the Maha-Pralay, again there is a fresh start for the humanity.

Same cycle of time happened a long time ago in the history of humankind, on a planet called 'Dharaa'. Humankind on this planet reached the apex of technological development. Humankind not only reaped the benefits of the scientific developments but also created the device for its own destruction.

The world was going to witness another world war, the final one. Vaivasvat, an immortal being and a visionary, foresees the inevitable war and the resulting planetary destruction. A true leader he was and under the guidance of the supreme lord Shree Vishnu, Vaivasvat formed a team comprising the most able people on the planet. Together they were called Saptarishi. Vaivasvat Manu and his wife Shraddha led the team of Saptarishi in the manufacture of a spaceship called Shree Vimana, and preserving the seeds and animal genomes. As the planet 'Dharaa' got destroyed because of a world war, all nine of them took the interstellar travel to reach their new home, Earth. On coming to the new found planet Earth, they used the seeds and animal genomes to recreate life on the planet.

The seeds turned into plants, plants into trees and trees into jungle. Likewise, various animal embryos were created which later flourished into healthy species. Humans were also created, and these humans colonized various continents of the planet Earth.

The Saptarishi - Gautam, Jamadagni, Vashistha, Atri, Kashyap, Bharadwaj and Vishwamitra - played a major role in creating a society. Besides being administrators, they were also the teachers for the newly formed society. They passed on Vedic knowledge to the humankind. They also moved across all the land masses and passed on their knowledge and expertise.

Lord Vishnu instructed Vaivasvat Manu, prior to the travel and before the start of his mission to save humanity, to not transfer any technology from the old planet to the new one. The intention behind this concealment was to prevent any misuse of the technology and to ensure the era of Manu, *Manvantar,* is as long as possible. Shree Vishnu wanted the humans in new manvantar to create, discover and invent all by themselves. Because ultimately, they *will* do it, and then inevitably they *will* misuse it. To delay the misuse, Shree Vishnu asked Vaivasvat Manu to not pass on the technology. Vaivasvat, his wife Shraddha and Saptarishi, did very well in hiding the scientific knowledge and technological advancements of the past world. In the same pursuit, they had to hide the Spaceship, Shree Vimana, away from the population to avoid its misused.

After surveying across several continents and water bodies, it was decided to hide the giant spacecraft in the uninhabited continent. The possibility of human settlement tends to be the minimum in that location. And this continent was the southern landmass, Himadri. In modern times, which would be called as Antarctica. The cloak location was as such, the Spaceship got completely covered in ice, in due course of time.

Several generations of Vaivasvat and Saptarishi descendants lived, flourished and died, but the Spaceship remained hidden. Until one day when Vaivasvat Manu had to use the same spaceship in order to make interstellar travel, to save the Vedic knowledge. Asuras had attacked the planet Earth.

Invaders capture and destroy the culture, literature, knowledge and pride of the civilization. This is how they gain control of the land and its dwellers. Vaivasvat Manu knew this very well and so he endeavoured to protect the Vedic manuscripts from the hands of Asuras. He undertook a journey to the Brahma Lok to hide the manuscripts.

Upon successfully completing his mission, he came back to the earth and handed over the spaceship to the then King of Kushasthali, Kakudmi. He gave it to Kakudmi not to use it, but to protect it.

"Never use it for your luxury or a selfish pursuit. However, you can take itsservice if it is required to protect your *Dharma*." Vaivasvat was very candid in giving the instructions and forbidding the misuse.

CONTENT

CHAPTER 1

NEW YORK

"True stories that have not been proved to be real have always been termed as fiction. The same is true for Plato's depiction of Atlantis. One day when human would find that submerged, lost city, it would no longer remain a fictional city," said Professor Doherty, as he ended his lecture.

Dr Edward Doherty, a sixty-year-old professor of archaeology, was a popular name in the anthropology and archaeological community. He had spent years looking for minute signs on the stones across the globe. Although he valued facts and truth, he was also a firm believer in the works of the ancient Greek philosopher Plato. It was Plato who had conceptualized the existence of Atlantis, a *fictional* ancient city that had achieved the heights of development. Following hidden mysteries and unravelling puzzles was his passion outside of work hours. Because of his passion, he had discovered many hidden treasures.

"But if Plato was so sure, why didn't he give the exact location?" asked one of the curious students, as the professor picked up his papers from the table.

"Good question, Jay. Let us discuss on this in our next lecture," said the professor as he walked towards the door.

Jay Swarney, a brilliant student in his final year of post-graduation, shared his own curiosity about archaeological ideas. He had his own struggle stories; juggling between his several part-time jobs apart from being a professor's assistant and a post-graduation student.

Jay followed the professor, swiftly moving towards him, and said, "Sir, the assignment on the Aryan movement and settlements is nearing its completion. When can I come to you to discuss pre-submission questions? I have some other queries as well."

"Were you able to establish the connection between Indo-European languages?"

Jay answered, "Yes sir, there are clearly visible links, and even in today's versions of these languages, the root words are closely related."

"Hmm... good... I would like to see those links in the assignment. And yes...come over to me after the classes. I need to discuss regarding an additional assignment."

Jay was not thrilled when he heard about the extra assignment. Rather, he was sad, as he wanted to free up some time for studying other subjects of his post-graduation.

"An additional... Sir?"

"Don't worry Jay. Don't worry Jay, this will be part of your assistantship and the government is providing grants for this paid assignment. Moreover, this would be an interesting one where you may be a part of a team of world class researchers."

While the talks went through, the legs moved towards Professor's cabin.

"Ok sure Sir. I shall see you later today," said Jay before moving back to his lecture theatre.

Jay came from a poor financial background and, because of this, he valued every bit of work that had monetary benefits linked to it. He was ready to work a couple more hours each day to earn some more dollars. And hence, his reluctance soon turned into an interest. It was also not that he did not like research work and assignments, but it was more to do with his overloaded schedule and zero time for himself. He was a curious student, and he loved diving deep into the sea of knowledge even to get a small pearl of information.

Jay walked briskly to come back to his lecture room. He did not want to miss any of the lectures. *The lecture should be starting any moment...* He was in his thoughts as he dashed and rubbed his shoulders with another man coming from the other side. Both felt the jerk as they looked at one another.

"S... sorry... Sir," said Jay as he looked towards the face of a middle-aged gentleman in formal attire with suits, ties and formal black shoes.

I have seen him somewhere... Is he Seth Kevin... the famous archaeologist?

"It's alright, I am fine," said that man and continued walking towards the gallery that led to Professor Doherty's cabin.

***

Professor Doherty had just settled on his chair when a familiar voice drew his attention.

"Hello Professor, I couldn't wait to see you when I heard the story of the submerged ancient city," said the man who had just entered the room of Edward Doherty.

"Hey Seth, I knew you would come. Have a seat," said the professor as he pulled out his notebook. Turning the pages of his notebook, he brought out a few notes, diagrams, and a hand-drawn map on the pages.

"This is what I was talking about, Seth. The discovery of the submerged city of Dwarka on the west coast of India has opened new chapters for our research work. Look at the rock structures of Dwarka and the city plan. This has a striking similarity with the so-called fictional city."

"Awesome. But the location of this place does not concur with the map of Atlantis," said Seth.

Seth Kevin was a famous author, who had written many books on the subject of archaeology. He had led many government projects for the US Archaeology & Anthropology Department. Although he was not a government employee, he worked with the government as a consultant and had access to many eminent authorities in the department. He gained much popularity for his research on *'cultural similarities of various civilizations that built pyramids across the world'*.

"True. That is something that's troubling me as well. But unless we go and look out, we cannot disregard other things that are coming out so boldly. Moreover, we have been to places like Malta, Gibraltar and Santorini, just following the map, yet we did not succeed," said Edward.

"So, are you planning to go there?" asked Seth.

"Yes, and I have already planned a team, and I see you as a part of it as well."

"Okay. What do you need from me?"

"We need you to accompany us to Dwarka. And use your handles in the government to get funds and papers, if you can."

Professor, I can't refuse you. You have been a great evangelist in this area of study. Your contributions to this knowledge area surpass what an entire batch could achieve.

Seth Kevin was indicating towards his own batch from the university. Prof Doherty had taught Seth Kevin, who had graduated from the same institution. That was some twenty years back when Edward Doherty was an Assistant Professor in the University.

"May I ask who all shall be in the team of this mission?"

"Three of my students, Jay, Patricia and Steve. And you and I. Steve and Patricia, who are trained divers, possess brilliant minds suitable for this task. They are also doing their papers on marine archaeology. Jay has an Indian background and is a good archaeologist as well. He knows the nitty gritty of the place. We shall be bringing in the local divers who have been to the bottom themselves."

"We should do the preparations for the journey," said Seth before departing from the university.

***

Later that day, Jay went to the Professor for the assignment feedback. As he entered the room, he could see two of his acquaintances, Patricia and Steve, having discussions with the professor. He could see some maps scattered on the table. On looking closely, he could see maps of India and the Arabian sea along with some photographs. The photos were not very unfamiliar; he had seen those before. Pointing towards the photos and the map, Jay couldn't help himself, but asked, "Are we going to see Atlantis?"

"Only if we are lucky enough, Mr Swarney," said Patricia.

"But you are right. This is your next assignment that I was talking to you earlier today," said Professor Doherty.

He further added, "We four of us and a consultant, Seth Kevin, would be heading to India in a couple of weeks."

"Was he Seth Kevin? The one who was here this morning."

"Did you meet him? He is a gem of an archaeologist. You all are going to learn a lot while working with him."

Jay nodded *yes* in the response.

All the three curious faces were delighted hearing a celebrity name in the team. They had read his papers and now they were about to work with him and that too, in an adventurous and interesting assignment.

"You all get your visa at the earliest. And keep me informed of the progress. As soon you have the travel documents, we shall fly," instructed the professor.

"In the meantime, I need you to read these papers, watch the documentaries I have forwarded to your inbox, and collect information that can help. These papers also include my earlier tours and research from similar sites in Malta and Santorini. Both places share similar traits like Dwarka, where we shall be heading to," he added further.

"Thank you, professor, for showing trust on me and giving me this opportunity to work on this project. It had always been my dream to work on similar marine archaeology. Ever since I saw the documentary by Juan Miguel on the discovery of a submerged port near Spanish coast, it was a dream to be part of a similar excursion," said Jay. He was too much excited as this would also serve as a value-add experience and help him find a job after his graduation.

"Perfect. But I need hard work and I need results," said the professor, looking at all of them.

CHAPTER 2

JAY

Jay Swarney came from a humble family background, being born to an immigrant family who moved from India for a better future. He was born and brought up in a small town called Woodbridge in the suburbs of New Jersey. After the death of his mother, he was the only bread earner of his family of three - his teenage sister, a disabled father and himself. Since his childhood days, he wanted to pursue the archaeological and historical studies just like his mother, who had worked at The National Museum of History. Although he was brilliant in studies, he was struggling with time, as he could not give sufficient time to prepare for interviews of the jobs he had applied for.

He had a long day after meeting Professor and his fellow team mates of upcoming assignment. He was jubilant a little after knowing his inclusion in the upcoming assignment, but there was a lot of scepticism within him, not letting him enjoy his present. His life had been very sordid so far and this sorrow deep within him was making all the excitement look like a dwarf.

The thoughts of taking care of his family, paying the bills and EMIs, making sure his sister gets a good life, and obtaining good marks in his own academics were some reasons for his anxiety attacks.

He was standing on his balcony and thinking about his life when he was brought back to *the present* by his sister's hand caressing his shoulders.

"What is troubling you dear brother," said his sister, Juhi.

"It is nothing, my little sister," said Jay, trying to force a smile on his face. But the enforced smile was noticed by Juhi who knew his brother better than anyone else.

"I know you, *bhaiya* , you are working hard to meet our ends."

Jay looked at Juhi and said, "you do not need to worry about all that. It is just that I am not getting any job offer despite appearing for so many interviews. Although, I have got an opportunity to work for an international archaeological assignment, but that is not enough for our growing needs."

"An international assignment! That is good news. What to worry then?"

"I will have wonderful experience working on the assignment. I know that. But I need a job after that. If I don't get any job, how can I fulfil my responsibilities?" said Jay in anguish.

Jay was only eighteen when his mother died of a cardiac attack. He had then just completed his junior college. His father was also not earning as he was paralysed below waist after a major road accident some ten years back. Jay had seen many tragedies in his brief life so far.

"Everything will be fine, *bhaiya*. Believe in Radhe-Krishna. They will do everything right. And now, come in. Dinner is waiting for you."

***

The next few days were hectic. All the team members had to prepare for the upcoming mission, thereby taking care of their personal and educational engagements. Jay, Patricia and Steve did their best to gather the knowledge from the internet and from the library, as per their capacity. But this was not enough; they also had to procure the instruments and devices that would help them in their work. And this included marine 4K cameras, large sized ROV devices that can crawl under the sea and capture images, and several other instruments for chipping and measurements.

The instruments were procured from the university and from the government archaeological department. They had the recommendation of reputed and celebrated intellectuals of the country.

While doing the preparations and gathering knowledge for his assignment, Jay got busy and, momentarily, he used to forget his misery. But one lightening thought brought his state back to anxiety. He was juggling between his polar emotions.

Oh Krishna! We will receive the result for Marine Tech later today.

He thought while getting some printouts from the University Library.

As he walked down the stairs of the library, Patricia stopped him. She was joyful and excited. She said, "Hey Jay, I got the offer from Marine Tech."

Jay had no instant emotion on his face. He looked at Patricia and let the information sync in. He said, "Congratulations. Who else are on the list?"

"It is only me. They have selected only one," said Patricia. She was delighted, especially because she was the only one to crack the test and interview.

That's the exact human nature. They derive happiness more from other's misery and less from their own accomplishment.

The news, however, sunk Jay several thousand feet below the surface in the sea of emotions. He was finding it hard to express anything at that moment. He walked out of the building without noticing the rain drops pouring down.

Patricia tried to stop him, but he could not hear any voice. He was walking away. The drizzle turned into a heavy downpour.

Water rolled down his cheeks. He was not sure it was rain or his tears. Or maybe he wanted to cry out, and this was the best place to do, where no one could see him or hear him crying. This was not the first time he had failed. But he was now tired of failing. Giving up was on his mind. He wanted to end all the sufferings. He kept walking towards the University gates, and later towards the cliff overlooking the mighty Hudson River.

***

Patricia knew Jay for the past five years. They were best friends. She sensed something was off about Jay but only realized what Jay was going through a bit late.

As the realization came that Jay could have got an anxiety attack, she hurried outside the library building. She found a university bicycle, hopped on it and rushed towards the gates. She knew Jay liked walking towards the cliff and so she followed him in the same direction. The rain had slowed down by now, but was enough to drain Patricia.

As she reached near the cliff point, she saw Jay standing very near to it.

"JAY, JAY," she shouted.

Jay looked back. He raised his hand, signalling Patricia to stop. Patricia, however, did not stop and went further towards him while speaking to him, "hey Jay, I want to talk to you. Let us talk. You are such a great person, why are you so much in stress? Let us talk. We will sort out your problems."

Jay by now was crying profusely. Patricia reached out to him, held his hands and pulled him towards herself and away from the cliff. She pulled him further and said, "what are you up to, Jay?"

"By now Jay had come to senses, but was still crying.

"I have so much of responsibilities, and every time I sense some hope and strength, I fail. Failure is sticking to me like these lines on my palm.

"Calm down, Jay. Calm down. Do not lose hope. As of now we have got such a wonderful assignment. Why not put our focus on this? And you have always said, what is there in destiny will happen," said Patricia as she held his hands.

She further continued, "and I am very sure there is something big in store for you. You only need to give it some time."

By now, rain had stopped, clouds disappeared, and the weather calmed down. Jay had also calmed down. He wiped off his eyes. And held Patricia's hand. Both of them walked to the bicycle.

***

The next morning, Patricia drove to Jay's house and picked him on the way to the University.

"How are you now, Jay?" asked Patricia, holding the steering wheel with one hand, looking at the road, and holding Jay's hand from the other.

Jay nodded his head, forcing a smile on his face, and said, "I am well now, Patricia."

"Did you share with your family?"

"Uh... No.." responded Jay. "I don't want to worsen their existing life issues. I can take care of myself."

"I know you can, but everyone needs someone to vent out their emotions. How often do you have such episodes?" asked Patricia.

"Last time I had was when I lost my mother. After we cremated her, I could not control myself."

"Do you realize so many individuals are part of you now? You are not alone. Promise me you would open up with me when you feel heavy. Friends are always there to take care. Remember, never go the way that leads you to loneliness," said Patricia.

Jay listened to each word carefully. He was happy from within that he matters to people around him.

Jay nodded his head, looking towards her.

***

Days passed and then approached the penultimate date before their departure.

The day before the start of their journey, a meeting was called by Professor Doherty with all his selected team members.

"So, dear friends, all set and ready for the adventure?" asked Prof Doherty.

"Yes Sir. Cannot wait more," Patricia responded, and saying out the words that echoed everyone's mindset.

"Good. You all would know Seth," the professor said, pointing towards him and added further, "he would be your guide in all the matters when I am unavailable."

"Sure Sir."

"But professor, why would you be not with us?" asked Jay. Patricia looked at Jay with a smile. She was happy that Jay was getting bonded with the assignment and devoting his time and interest to something fruitful.

"I shall be available, but as you know, for every pilot, there's a co-pilot and for every captain there's a vice-captain. Likewise, there has to be a delegation in place to handle any unwanted situation," answered the professor.

As Prof Doherty was speaking, he received an email from Jay. His smart watch beeped. Professor touched the screen only to be surprised as he saw sender as Jay.

"Jay, you are here and sending an email to me," the professor smiled, showing his watch to Jay. That confused Jay, as he had no idea of any email that he had sent or scheduled.

"No...No... I haven't," responded Jay.

By this time, the professor opened the email, and it read:

Professor, do not go on this mission

"What short of joke is this?" "Are you kidding me?" the professor asked, appearing irritated after reading Jay's email.

"But Professor, I have not sent any email. I believe someone has hacked my email or something.

"Okay, if that is the case, let us ignore this," the professor trusted one of his best students.

But Jay was confused and had a sense of fear as to why anyone would stop them from the mission. He had no answer, but only questions.

"Ok, dear friends, have a good luck for the mission. Have a good night's sleep and let us meet at the airport tomorrow."

CHAPTER 3

INDIA

Five of the team members arrived at Ahmedabad airport in the morning hours. Except Jay, all others had landed on the Indian soil for the first time. They had never come to the subcontinent either, despite having studied about the ancient civilizations like Harappa and Indus Valley.

The recent excavations of Sinauli in the northern part of India was another site Professor Doherty was interested to visit, provided he gets time off from his current assignment. And that time off was only possible if they hit the gold early in their search. Sinauli, a small town in the state of Uttar Pradesh, was in a land lying between two major rivers of the country–Ganga and Yamuna. This site gained attention for its Bronze age solid disk wheel cart, which was interpreted as remnants of Mahabharata age chariots.

Although Sinauli was one of the topmost excavation sites Professor had on his visit list, right now he was all engrossed in the thoughts of Dwarka. He knew that Dwarka was also a city of mythological importance to the people of India, and it belonged to the same period in the mythological history as Sinauli.

Professor Doherty and his team had their first place of stay at Ahmedabad. They had appointments with some Archaeological Survey experts, a famous historian named Dr Kamal Parekh and a Hindu religious guru named Swamy Shankar Acharya of *Govind*

Sansthanam.

As they moved into the airport transfer van, the professor said to his team, "friends, let us relax and rejuvenate the rest of the day. Come out of jet lag and feel this land. From tomorrow, we are going to be on our mission."

"Yes Sir, but the heat is on..." said Steve as he was sweating even inside an air-conditioned vehicle. The summer of India was getting started and residents of New York were feeling its effect.

"This is what India is like, and especially Ahmedabad. But do not worry. Dwarka would be cooler, although a little humid," said Jay. Jay had Indian roots and so he had some idea about its climate, culture and language.

"Hmm, yes, you would have to take the heat to glitter," said Professor Doherty.

All this time Seth Kevin was silently observing the city, the hustle bustle of streets, the busy traffic and the sudden appearance of bullock carts, children running with loads of weight on their bulging shoulder bags, people shouting religious chants while moving in saffron clothes. Everything was looking alien, but interesting to him.

"This trip is going to be a memorable one," said Seth.

"You bet," said professor.

"Okay friends, so you all should be having the schedule of our next two days' stay at Ahmedabad. Hope you all have gone through. We shall stick to that schedule, but I am yet to distribute the ownership to all of you," said the professor to his teammates.

By this time, they reached their hotel.

As they walked in to the hotel, Patricia held Jay's hand and said, "how are you now?"

"I am feeling good and relaxed. Thank you for holding my hand when I needed the most," replied Jay with gratitude in his voice and eyes.

***

Checking-in into their rooms, each of them went to bed. The tiredness and the body clock could not resist getting some sleep. In the evening, all the team members gathered in the restaurant of the hotel. This was their time to group up and plan for the upcoming mission.

Professor Doherty looked towards each of them, Jay, Patricia, Steve and Seth. He smiled and said, "hope you all had a good nap. And more sleep guaranteed for the night. But before that, let us discuss the plan."

As they were discussing, food and drinks were served on their table. Professor had pre-ordered from the menu. He did not want to waste any time on the discussion of food.

Everyone nodded as an acknowledgement.

Professor drew out his notebook. Turned few pages to bring up the page having the plan for the next two days.

"We have to meet three sets of people - Historians, Archaeologists and Religious Guru. Seth, no one knows history better than you and you are the right person to ask the right question to Dr Parekh. He has a vast knowledge of Indian history. And you need to gather all the information about Dwarka that is not available in the books or over the internet."

"Sure, Professor. And where will I find him?" asked Seth.

"I have already talked to him and got his time. You can meet him tomorrow at the University of Gandhinagar, Dept. of History. He has the background information, and he is expecting to see you by tomorrow noon," answered Professor Doherty.

"Ok."

"Jay and Steve, you should meet the knowledgeable and revered Hindu Guru, Swamy Shankar. He is a learned man and is a regular visitor to the states for lectures on religion and spirituality. Gather as much as you can from him. Know the religion and understand the importance of Dwarka."

Professor further added, "again, I have already got his appointment. You need to meet him tomorrow morning. Do not be late. Reach before 9 AM. Here is the address." And the Professor passed on the card having the address of Govind Sansthanam.

"And what task do I have, sir?" asked Patricia.

"You would go to the Office of the Indian Archaeological Survey. And you should meet the officials to find out what artifacts have been recovered so far. What story the artifacts tell? Further to gathering the information, you also need to procure the permit to dive into the submerged city."

"Oh. That's the toughest part of all three," said Patricia.

"Do not worry. I shall be with you."

"That is great. Thank you, Professor."

"Questions?"

"Not as of now," said Jay, and all nodded their head.

"Fine, good luck. Have this delicious Indian meal."

Everyone was excited, but now they knew that the work was heavy and they need tremendous effort with smartness. They had only two days to learn what people learn in years.

***

Next day, Jay and Steve started early. Before 9 AM, they had to reach their destination, which was about twenty kilometres away. They had already got a taste of Ahmedabad road-traffic and they did not want to get late at their first meeting with Guru Swamy Shankar.

In a timely manner, they arrived at Govind Sansthanam. Guru Swamy Shankar was waiting for them after completing his morning prayer.

"Welcome to the land of Lord Krishna, my brothers from America," said *Swamy ji*.

Swamy Shankar was referred to as *Swamy ji* by his disciples.

"Namaste Swamy ji" responded Jay, with his folded hands. Steve, having little knowledge of Indian culture, also gestured similarly.

Swamy ji said, "Please be seated," and continued, "What brings you here?"

"Swamy ji, we are here to know more about Dwarka, the city that we shall be seeing and also the one that we cannot see," responded Jay. Jay was a little hesitant, but he mustered his courage and regained his originality.

Swamy ji, with a narrow smile, said, "I like your curiosity and your clarity of words."

He further added, "and yes you are right. Dwarka, that used to be ruled by Shree Krishna has evolved and moved. It used to be few kilometres away from the present shoreline. But with the change of yug, *Samudra Dev* engulfed that magnificent city. Sea approached and filled up the city. Consequently, population shifted away from the flooded place. The city that we see now, is the city of Kaliyug."

"Swamy ji, does that mean the present Dwarka did not exist

during Shree Krishna's reign?" asked Steve.

"Oh, it did, my friend. This was what you call a suburban city. The downtown, as you refer in America, was the Dwarka city that got flooded."

"So, you mean Dwarka was such a big city in those ancient days?"

"It sure was. After all, it was the business hub, a major harbour of the world, a cultural and business centre of the era."

"Swamy ji, can you also help us with some dates... as when all this happened?" asked Jay.

"Kaliyug started about five thousand years ago. And the major portion of Dwarka sunk around that time during the turn of the Yug. After all, the people of Kaliyug do not deserve to see and feel the purity and magnificence of that divine place. So, it was required for the yug to progress."

"And Swamy ji, why do you think we do not deserve to see that?"

"The sin and evil are all around. When there is sin and wickedness in the thought, the technology and capability have to be hidden. That is the process of nature to balance itself. Or else humanity would have misused those things."

Jay struggled to believe how science could be so advanced in the past and asked, "so, were there advanced technologies?"

"Oh yes, Mr Swarney. You see, this is actually a cyclic process. If you see long back, during the start of the manvantar, the world had all the devices and technologies that today's humans cannot even think of."

"What is manvantar, *guruji*," asked Steve.

Guruji smiled and said, "In the Hindu scriptures time has been divided into manvantars. Each manvantar is a long period of millions of years and has many *chatur-yugas* within them. Each manvantar is under the leadership of a king know as Manu. In the current manvantar Manu is Vaivasvat Manu. The next manvantar after the Pralay would be under the reign of Savarni Manu."

Guruji stopped for a moment, looked at Jay and said, "Mr Swarney, you seem to share your name with the next Manu this world would see, the Savarni Manu," and Guruji broke into a laughter.

The two audiences were not very amused but were keeping their ears open to catch all the knowledge that was being radiated on to them.

Swamy ji was very clear in his thoughts. Without blinking his eyelids, he answered. He knew what he was saying, and he was genuinely interested in the research of the American fellows. He was enjoying their curiosity and questions.

On the other side, Jay and Steve, like hungry animal were swallowing as much as they could grab.

They kept on taking notes while Swamy ji opened up his knowledge gates. Swamy ji also suggested that they read Mahabharat and Bhagvat Gita.

***

Seth Kevin, with the task of understanding the history of Dwarka, reached the University of Gandhinagar. He was on time to meet Kamal Parekh. Unlike his team mates Jay and Steve, he had good knowledge of the subject for which he was going to interview. And Kamal Parekh knew and had read Seth. He admired the intellect Seth belonged to, and the same was true for Kamal.

"Welcome to the land of spirituality and yoga, Dr Kevin," Kamal greeted as he saw a foreigner enter his department. Although he never met him personally, he had seen him in various webinars and in the pages of journals.

"Pleasure to see you, Dr Parekh. I was reading your book, *History Underground* a week back. I must admit, I had never read anything like that in recent times," said Seth.

Seth was knowledgeable, and a disciplined and hardworking researcher. He knew the importance of doing the home-work. He had read all he could in the brief span of time he got after knowing about the mission.

We get the right answer by asking the right question. And no one knew better than Seth about this.

"Thank you. So, what can I do for you, Dr Seth?"

"I have read about the history of ancient India, but I have not found much about Dwarka on the web or in the books. I feel that researchers have written very little about Dwarka," said Seth.

"That is right. There is a lot of mythology in this place, but very less of history. And you know, there is a fine line separating the two," said Kamal.

"I understand. Many things that appear myth sometimes find a significant place in history. Whereas there are cases where historical events have found similarity to mythological accounts. I am here to remove the dust on top of those historical artifacts and mythical texts."

"I see."

After a pause Kamal continued, "The city that we see now, and including the Dwarkadhish Temple, dates back to about 500 BC.

Although the exact date is unknown because this city saw many invaders and destroyers. The present-day temple was rebuilt in the 16th century, after the older one was destroyed by Mahmud Begada. There are some copper artifacts that have references back to the fifth and sixth century BC that establish the prospering city of Dwarka."

"Interesting. So, you do not have any history on Dwarka prior to 500 BC?" asked Seth.

"Unfortunately, No. History that is written so far stops at 500 BC. What goes back beyond that is archaeology," responded Kamal with a big smile.

"I knew. Archaeology goes beyond history," Seth echoed the smile and some laughter.

Seth utilized the remaining time learning about the local and national historical facts and interpretations. He was a wise man and knew that historical facts are also interpretations, so no reason to ignore others.

CHAPTER 4

THE MUSEUM

The office of the Indian Archaeological Survey was not only a government office but also housed a museum. This museum had all the relics and artifacts that were excavated out of the lost city of Dwarka and nearby areas. Professor Doherty had read about the museum and had also communicated with the department officials prior to his arrival.

Professor had an appointment with the survey officer, Mr Alok Singh. He helped Professor Doherty and Patricia with their many questions before taking a walk through the museum.

As they moved along the museum corridor, Professor Doherty and Patricia could see the rocks of various shapes and sizes that were retrieved out of the excavations. Alok explained to them about the significance of those rocks, along with the time period those were supposed to be from. Many of those were round shaped grind-stones, and some were square shaped building blocks. Whereas very few were like written tablets, as if those served as some kind of scriptures or texts of the era.

"Has this script been read?" asked Patricia.

"Oh yes, this is Sanskrit. All you see here are Vedic mantras written on these rocks," answered Alok.

He continued, "you can find these mantras in Hindu religious texts."

"Mr Alok, have you found anything, any artifact, that you feel out of the box? I mean, anything that should not be out there?" Professor

Doherty asked a rather intriguing question. But he was the kind of scholar who researched on things that are out of the normal. And this was one of the many questions he surely asked in his research visits.

This question took Alok by surprise, as he was not expecting it. There was a sense of uneasiness around him. He wanted to reveal something, but also wanted to hide. He was not sure how people would perceive his interpretation. But somehow, he found words and said, "We have some tablets lifted up only a few days back. All those have Sanskrit mantras inscribed on them, and that is what was expected, but..."

Alok paused and took a deep breath before continuing, "there is one among those tablets, that have Roman letters also inscribed in between the Sanskrit letters."

"Hmm... Okay. But why is that so significant to you? Over time, we have seen many such instances where original inscriptions get deformed, unwritten or modified," said Professor Doherty. He was finding this just normal.

"That is right, Professor Doherty. But there's a graphical representation that would certainly raise eyebrows," said Alok.

"That is interesting. We cannot wait more to witness that piece of relic."

"Oh, yes," said Alok in confirmation and added, "please come this way," and he led them into a room full of rocks scattered all around.

"These are the recent findings and are yet to put on the display," he added.

From the floor, he picked up an ordinary looking square piece of rock and removed the dust from it. Some letters were engraved on that rock.

"You see, here," Alok holding the rock in his left hand and pointing his right-hand index finger at the inscription. "It is written in Sanskrit and it reads *kalo asmi loka kshaya krit pravriddho lokan samahartum iha pravrittah*. And look below this. It reads *www* dot something, which is broken and not readable. Further, look at this graphical inscription. Can you figure this out as what this is?" Alok asked.

"Yes, I can see. This looks like a QR code and a web address," said Professor Doherty.

"Exactly. Now the question is- how on earth QR code existed 5000 years back?" Alok was excited to throw his surprise at the foreign visitors.

Professor was amazed to see such an out-of-place object. He could not believe his eyes at once but later held that rock to look closer in to it.

"And did you read this code?" asked Professor.

"No, we could not. The QR is broken... here at the right bottom corner," said Alok, pointing towards the broken and incomplete piece of rock.

"And what does this Sanskrit writing mean?" asked Professor Doherty. He was puzzled, but he was used to these encounters and he knew how to solve them.

"This is a part of a *shloka* from The Bhagvat Gita. It means - I am mighty Time, the source of destruction that comes forth to annihilate the worlds. In these words, the Supreme Lord is saying to Arjuna, the great Mahabharata warrior, that Lord himself is the mighty time. This is only a part of the complete verse. I believe the other half of the verse would have been broken out of the rock," explained Alok.

Alok further said, "like many other rocks excavated from under the sea, this also contains the Gita verses, just that it is little different from others."

"So, you mean there are other rocks found which contains similar inscriptions?" Patricia said, holding the rock in her hand.

"Yes, there are many. All have Gita verses inscribed in Sanskrit language and script. And that is expected given the age these rocks were carved out."

"And are you sure this piece of rock is 5000 years old?" asked Professor Doherty.

"This rock has been excavated much below the other rocks that have other verses of Gita. We have also evaluated it using stratigraphy and have found it to be of that age."

"Interesting. So, you have ruled out the case of this piece getting scribed in the modern day." Professor **Doherty** held the rock and asked.

He further asked, "Can we take a photograph of this rock?"

"Yes, Sure. Please go ahead." Alok did not see any issue sharing the details and information to the scientific community across the border.

***

Patricia and Professor Doherty had an interesting day. So was for all others in the team. They were excited as they had learnt something new that day. During their evening gathering, everyone wanted to share their story. Professor, however, was silent and within himself trying to assimilate what was served to him during the day.

Patricia was equally puzzled and put forth her unsolved mystery.

She said to her team, "friends, we met with something very strange, which was not supposed to be there."

"What is that, Patricia?" asked Jay.

"This piece of rock we saw at the Archaeology Department that had Sanskrit inscriptions and had an image sculpted on it that looked akin to a QR code. Moreover, it had an inscription that looked like a web address. The strange about it is, back then, such QR code or similar art did not exist."

"Are we sure it is from that age?" asked Steve.

"That is what Archaeology Department has found," answered Patricia.

Professor interrupted her saying, "we have asked for the Lab reports. Let us see what reports suggest."

Professor looked towards Patricia and said, "Can you send the picture of this QR code to our AI Lab in the University and ask them to reconstruct the broken part to see what this QR code is possibly referring to?"

"Sure, Sir. I will send across this photograph for processing."

Professor further continued the conversation, "and how was your day, Seth?"

"I got to know more about the local history. It was more of the same stuff I had expected, Professor. The recorded history dates back to only two-and-a-half millennia, whereas this place existed for more than five thousand years. Yes, one thing of some importance that I came across was the palm leaf manuscripts. These manuscripts on the leaf have a life of around four hundred years. But people here have been preserving the ancient knowledge by writing the same inscription on the fresh palm leaves. And they do this, generation after generation, by re-writing historical anecdotes," said Seth.

"That is interesting. Do you have any picture of those manuscripts?" asked the Professor.

"Oh yes, Professor. I did click a couple of them after their permission."

"Great. Excellent stuff, Seth."

"Jay and Steve, what stories did you unravel?" asked Professor Doherty.

"The mystical guru supports the idea that Dwarka used to be a much bigger and larger city than what it is today. As per him, most of that ancient city is now down under the water, and a very small portion is on land. He believes that what we see today is just one suburb, and the downtown is lost.

"I hope you all enjoyed your part of work so far. Let us explore further for one more day before we move to Dwarka," said the professor.

The team continued in their search for facts and truth and drafted their reports before packing their bags. Their stay in Ahmedabad was brief one but gave them a taste of what food they were going to be served in the days to come.

CHAPTER 5

DWARKA

With many unanswered questions, the team travelled to Dwarka. Professor, immersed in his thought, was still trying to solve the puzzle he had come across. Finding a little rationality in even the irrational was the professor's way to justice. He gave every opportunity to any possibility. And because of this, he was still trying to figure out the two things. First, Jay's hacked email before their departure from the US. And second, the mysterious rock piece from Dwarka.

The weather was much cooler as compared to Ahmedabad. The cool breeze from the sea made the team at comfort, although the humidity was making it tough for them to remain dry.

On their arrival in Dwarka, they met with another American team who were reconnoitring the place. That American team of marine archaeologists and environmentalists had already taken a couple of dives into the ancient site. That team was led by Dr Stephan Carter. He was a marine archaeologist and was a well-known name in the field. Professor Doherty was not unknown either. Both had worked together on a project earlier.

"Anything unusual, Steph, in this place?" asked Professor Doherty at their meeting.

"This is a good place for people like us, Ed. There is definitive evidence of a prosperous city that stood out there in the past. I must tell that they were very advanced and their civil engineering was as developed as we are today," responded Dr Carter.

He further continued after a momentary pause, "it is submerged in water, that too highly saline, for more than five thousand years. And still the foundation is as strong as any new building of the modern era would have."

"We would like to be part of your diving team, if that is okay with you?" asked the professor.

"Oh sure. We do not have any problem. You can join us when we venture out to the sea tomorrow." Stephan was more than happy to support another team in the pursuit of knowledge.

***

The next day, they started early. Both the team ventured in to the Arabian sea from the Dwarka city coast. They hired a private boat. It was another day at sea for the team and they were prepared for it. They ventured approximately 3 nautical miles in to the sea before dropping their anchors.

Patricia and Jay, being the divers, joined the other divers. While they took the dip, other team members along with Professor were using the Sonar signals to map the seafloor and look out for any abnormality in the underwater structures.

The divers had phones attached to their ear and were constantly in touch with the surface.

"Professor, this is amazing," said Jay.

"What do you see, Jay?" asked Professor Doherty.

"Sir, the walls of the ancient city, the passages of the city, the ruins of the building. Everything." Jay was excited.

For an archaeologist, nothing can excite more than the rocks hidden under for ages. The view of those rocks that once were part of a long-lost human civilization was a treat to the eyes. Jay couldn't resist explaining every view he was having. He was closely looking into the rocks and boulders to search for any inscription or an art from the past. Finding either of these would add to his reward. Looking at the vastness of the submerged ruins, he knew he had a lot of work to do in the coming days.

On the surface, Professor and other teammates were equally elated. They had come so far to witness this and now they are just on top of something they believed a probable candidate for Atlantis. Professor moved to another cabin in the boat. This cabin had the monitors to see through the underwater camera. Dr Carter and his team had taken the camera underwater and they could see and record all that was lying below.

"Wow, look at that pathway, Professor. It clearly seems like a roadway from the past, with the rock walls on either side of it," said Steve.

"Hmm... looks amazing."

"Can we get the full map of this place?" Professor asked the technician who was handling the equipment on the boat.

"We are working on that, sir. As soon as we have it done, you shall have it."

"Oh, thank you," said the Professor, but thinking as why do they take so long to draw the map? He got up from his seat and paced on to the deck. He was behaving very impatiently, just like a kid.

Professor Doherty was a senior person in the industry and was very patient, but he could not hold his nerves out of his desperation to explore and obsession towards his work.

"Professor, something written over here," the telephonic voice of Patricia reached the professor.

Professor Doherty ran to the telephone device and said, "what is it? Can you describe it, please?"

"This is a sizeable piece of wall. Seems like some Sanskrit sentences are written and there are some drawings engraved as well."

"Good find. Please click those pictures."

"Professor, there are more of these drawings. We are capturing these."

Professor was happy. They were progressing on the assignment for which they travelled to the other side of the globe.

"Great," said Professor and looked towards Seth and continued, "we have lots of work to be done going through those captures."

Patricia, Jay and the other divers continued their search and exploration for the remaining part of the day, taking some rest on the surface intermittently. By the late afternoon, they had almost captured a good area under the sea.

***

Back in the hotel in Dwarka, the Professor's room had become an archaeological workshop. The team was scouring through the photographs and the videos. They had also brought some pieces of small rocks from the sea.

"Sir, most of these Sanskrit texts are from the Bhagvat Geeta," said Jay. He could read the Sanskrit script and also searched that Sanskrit text over the internet to find out what it meant.

"Okay, and how about others?" asked Seth.

"Some are street directions to important buildings of that city, like Administrative Block, King's Palace, Warrior's practice arena and others."

"Good to know they were so developed to have this setup in

their city, back five thousand years," the professor could not stop himself from praising the lost civilization. He was, in a way, telling to himself that *this is indeed the Atlantis.*

Most eyes were busy with the photographs on their laptop.

Suddenly, Patricia almost jumped off her seat. She had received an email from the Artificial Intelligence Department of their university. And as she opened the email and read it, she could not resist her awe, and said, "hey all, look here... this is becoming too thrilling to handle now..."

"Why? What happened?" asked Jay.

"The broken QR code that we sent to the department for investigation turns out that it is a link to our department's website. And...."

"And what?"

"It is the web page where Professor Doherty had published some articles related to similarity in the design of modern-day dams and those found in ancient Indian sites."

Everyone raised their eyebrows after hearing the mysterious finding.

Professor Doherty went in a deep thought and said, "that article I had published with an architect friend about ten years ago, and it is not a work that I am proud of. I could never prove many of the assumptions mentioned in that paper."

"But Sir, the question is still unanswered. How on earth is that QR code come in the ancient relics?" asked Seth.

"Yes, true. Moreover, the reports sent by the Indian Archaeological Team suggest the age of that piece of rock as somewhere around five-thousand years," suggested Professor.

The excitement of the room suddenly came down, and the air around became gloomy with a lot many questions floating. They were getting only surprises and no answers to their curious questions.

"Okay friends. Let us call it a day. I know you all have done a lot of hard work. And we have more to do tomorrow. I will suggest get some rest."

"Sure Professor. Good night."

And the team dispersed.

Back in his room, alone, looking at his laptop, Professor Doherty opened his department website. He navigated to his long-forgotten article and read the article one more time.

Is this a sign? Is some force pushing us somewhere? What is happening?

Professor maintained his calmness when he was with others. But when alone, he was struggling with the questions from within. Just like a duck floating over water looks so calm, but under the water, it is working hard to remain floating.

And that is what was required of him. An anchor cannot be shaky, it has to be firm to hold the ship.

***

The next day was almost the same until noon. Divers and researchers below the surface were scouring the sea floor, looking for rocks. Those rocks seemed more precious than diamonds.

It was just minutes past noon when one of the divers found another piece of rock with some Sanskrit verses and a map on it.

Like all the artifacts, this rock reached Professor's hand when brought out of the sea. Professor called upon his Sanskrit expert, Mohan Trivedi, whom he had hired from Dwarka. Mohan Trivedi was a Post-Graduate in Sanskrit language. He worked as a freelancer providing language support to the foreign and Indian researchers. His freelancing work took off very well after the discovery of the sunken city of Dwarka. He was a humble and intelligent man.

"What does this Sanskrit texts suggest, Mr Mohan?" asked the professor to the Sanskrit expert, handing over the square rock of side about 7 inches.

Mohan carefully held the rock, removed some soil from it and brought the rock closer to his lens.

"Sir, this suggests of some geographical location like an instruction for a map..."

"Can you please translate it literally, Mr Mohan?"

"Yes Professor. It reads - *sa divya vastu kushasthali paschime dasham yojanam...* This translates in English to - that divine object (or land) of kushasthali is ten yojan to the west."

He further added, "and after this, the piece of rock is broken."

"So, this refers to a piece of land or an object?" asked Professor Doherty.

"Sir, not very sure about that. It says *vastu*, that means object, but it also refers to the name of Kushasthali, which is a land reference. It may mean both."

"Okay, and what does this unit yojan refers to?" asked the Professor.

"Sir, this is an ancient measurement unit which has been used in Indian religious texts. Although there are many interpretations of the exact equivalent in current units. But the one widely accepted is ... one yojan equivalent to eight miles," replied Mohan.

"And as you can see, sir, there is also some part of a map here," said Mohan.

"Yes, I see. It seems as if water surrounds this piece of land which is a circular in shape on all sides, and three big pieces of land masses on three sides," said Professor.

Mohan responded, "yes, sir. It seems as if this is an island surrounded by water and three gigantic land masses. The land masses seem to be a far distance as compared to the size of the island. But there is an equal probability that this is a circular shaped object."

Professor loved solving puzzles. And every piece of rock had its own story behind the puzzle engraved on it. This map and the instruction had aroused Professor's appetite for problem solving. He looked towards Steve and said, "Steve, can you please capture this in the cam and process the photo?"

"Sure, Sir."

And Steve did the same. In a moment they had a clear photograph of the map, after applying digital filters and taking help from artificial intelligent software.

"Wow, amazing! Is this a map of the Arabian Sea?" elated Steve could not stop his excitement.

"May be, maybe not. These land masses have similar shapes, like the Arabian Peninsula in the west and Iran-Pakistan in the north and India in the east," said Professor.

He further continued with his suggestion, "Now, can you pull out the geographical map and drop a pin on the point eighty miles west of this GPS location?"

"Here it goes... and sir, this is somewhere in the waters, in the middle of the Arabian Sea."

"Let me see," said the professor, getting closer to the monitor.

Without his glasses, he had to bend closer to the screen to see better. He was so excited that he could not spend time to pick up his glasses on the table at the corner of the cabin.

"So, as per this rock, there may be a city named Kushasthali in the Arabian Sea. Good to know that we have one more prospective site," said the professor with a mild smile as he moved towards his glasses.

***

Back in the hotel, Professor Doherty received the subsurface map of the ruined and submerged city of Dwarka. He called a meeting of his team members to put down the research and finding. And he addressed the team.

"Friends, we have received the bottom structural map. This looks very much like a modern city, with criss-cross roads. This place has also presented us with some mysterious pieces of information and evidences. We would continue scouring under water city, but before that let us search for the place suggested by this rock piece," said Professor Doherty, pointing his finger towards the rock piece they discovered in the morning.

"I see. So, what is next, Professor?" asked Seth.

Professor responded and added further, "This place has given many clues. Has thrown light on the advanced civilization this had hosted in the history. We need to study this information that we have collected and prepare the full report of this place. But now, let us dive eighty miles away."

***

The next day, the team did not waste any of their time after the breakfast and headed directly to the water. The local divers also accompanied them, but with one condition that they would not venture more than 100 nautical miles in the sea. This was their norm to not venture more given the nature of turbulence the sea has. Professor Doherty knew that the pin on the map as per the location prescribed on the tablet of Dwarka was approximately 90 nautical miles from the coast of Dwarka in the west direction. He was, hence, good with the condition of the local divers.

All the 8 people, including the three local divers, were on board a large boat. The speed of the boat was around 30 miles an hour, and hence they expected to reach their area of search in about three-hour time.

"I hope you all are having a good time here," asked the professor to his students, Steve and Patricia. While both were in the saloon along with the Professor, Jay was standing on the deck and feeling the cool air breeze immersed in deep thought.

"Yes, Professor. Rocks are speaking here," said Patricia.

"Very true. I hope we get more interesting finds later on this tour," responded Professor Doherty. He then moved to the deck to check with Jay.

Jay was looking towards the horizon opposite to the climbing sun. In his memory, he was walking the lane that had all the questions and emotions he encountered since the assignment began. His anxiety attack, the email, the tablet and the professor's article were knocking his mind, each one asking to solve the mystery of its existence. Suddenly, a hand rested on his right shoulder, and he came back from his daydream, a little surprised and a little frightened, suddenly awoken by someone. This was the professor's hand.

"Is anything troubling you, Jay?" asked Professor Doherty.

"No... No Sir... It is not a trouble; I was just lost in the maze that is changing its shape every moment."

"Very much understandable. Life would give you many puzzles that would seem unsolvable, but just be watchful and keep re-calibrating every parameter before making a move. Just make the best effort and the result would surely come your way," said Professor, finger-combing his hair, which was furling with the wind.

"But Sir, we have never got so many questions, one after the other, all becoming humongous day by day. Have never faced such... is this a sign?" asked Jay.

"If it is a sign, let us face it. And unless you take a dip, you could never find if it a pearl or a pebble."

The boat was cruising at a high speed, splashing the water on to the deck. They were about to reach their dropped pin-point.

"It is only a couple more miles," said Seth, and he approached the two on the deck.

*****

As they reached the pinned-location, they could feel the turbulent waters under their boat. The wind was stronger than other parts of the sea. The water waves were striking the deck and splashes of drops sprinkled over the people on the deck.

"Let us put down the anchors," shouted the Professor, directing his voice towards the uniformed ship crew.

One of the crew members nodded in acknowledgement and went ahead with his work.

"Team, let us gather and get ready for our work," said the Professor.

In the next 15 minutes, all of them were ready with their tools, notepads, or the diving gears.

Patricia and Jay, being trained divers and marine archaeologists, were an obvious choice for the people to go below the surface. Two of the local divers who carried cameras and metal detecting devices accompanied them. In one of the saloons of the boat, other team members set up the devices.

All the divers took the plunge and were in a depth of the sea in the next few minutes.

The colour of water around them changed every few minutes; from light blue at the surface to navy blue and then to dark shades of grey as they went deeper. The ocean current below the surface was much stronger than they had anticipated. The water current pushed them several feet away from the point they had dived. All of them safely and comfortably landed on the ocean floor and started their scouring activity.

"Hey Professor, we can see lots of boulders and ship-wreckages in here," said Jay on the phone.

"Keep looking for the rocks," said Professor Doherty, looking towards the screen that had video streaming from one of the cameras of the divers.

Looking for the rocks, Patricia and Jay moved away from the divers. They were trying to cover as much as possible.

Patricia looked towards her left and excitedly raised her hand to get the attention of Jay. As Jay looked towards her, she beckoned to her left. On her left, in about a hundred meters, they could see an underwater mountain.

"Wow, there seems to be a mountainous structure. We are going over there," said Jay over the phone.

"Take care of yourself, guys," said Steve on the microphone.

***

Mountains on the ocean floor are not that rare, but are also not very common. Seeing one, raised the heart-beats for many divers, out of excitement and curiosity. The two archaeologists moved closer to the mountain foot and could see small fishes moving near the algae on the rock surface. They scratched some algae out of it to uncover the skin of the mountain and rubbed off some chips of the rock. Collecting the chips, they swam along the circumference of the mountainous base. Suddenly they stopped, landed their feet on the floor and were staring at a big cavity on the mountain.

"Hey guys, there is a cave down here," informed Patricia to the team above the surface.

"How big is it? Can you go in there?" asked the Professor.

"Oh yes, we can. This is sufficiently big for us to walk in there with our head upright," responded Patricia.

She further added, "we are going in."

Jay was the first to enter that *black hole,* followed by Patricia. Moving further, Jay noticed some rock drawings partially visible and partly covered with algae. He used his knife to wipe off the greenery and expose the rock painting. The rock painting was very faded and not easily recognizable. But they could make from the style of drawing that it was indeed a human-made.

"Click those Patricia," said Jay, and moved further. Patricia was busy with her camera. Suddenly, she felt an enormous blow of water current coming from inside the cave. Jay had moved away from the current and was standing near the cave wall, but Patricia could not escape. She was thrown several meters away. The blow of the current was so huge that Patricia was unconscious for a few moments.

"Hey, Patricia, are you okay?" asked Jay, rushing towards her.

Patricia was lying on the floor. Jay reached out to her, shook her hand and her upper torso to allow some breathing to happen. Within the next few seconds, Patricia opened her eyes, breathing air from the cylinder. She looked towards Jay. "What was that?" she asked.

"I do not know, some kind of sea beast, or may be trapped air. But how are you?" asked Jay.

"I am okay, just feeling pain in my abdomen," she responded.

"Let me take you to the surface," he said and helped Patricia to stand on her feet and swim in water. He supported her, and both went up towards the surface.

***

Seth pulled out Patricia with his right hand as she came out and held the iron bars of the stairs attached to the boat.

"Thank god, you are safe," said Seth, who was silent all this time and was following up every step of theirs underwater, through the camera and the phone.

Patricia removed her headgear and the oxygen pipe and took a deep breath while lying on the floor of the deck.

"How are you now?" asked Jay.

"I am alright," she responded.

"What was that?" he asked.

By now, the team gathered on the deck.

"I don't know. May be some kind of animal or a blow of water current. But whatever it was, it was forceful," said Patricia.

"Okay, good that you are fine but I'd suggest you take rest remainder of the day and assist the team on the surface," said Professor.

He further added, "and I will be accompanying Jay underwater."

Professor was the only other marine archaeologist in the team who was a diver as well. In fact, he was an expert diver just that he was a little old and got tired very soon. But he had no other option left. He had to join Jay and two were needed to carry out the study successfully. And in the back of his mind, he had made himself prepared as a backup resource in case of any injury or mishap.

Without losing much time, Professor Doherty was ready with all the diving gears. Jay and the Professor dived into the ocean.

***

Professor Doherty followed Jay. Both were soon at the same place - the mouth of the cave. Professor looked at the uncovered piece of rock painting before moving deeper in to the cave.

The darkness of the cave increased. They had already turned on the lights of their helmets. Little and medium size fishes swam along with them. Crabs and small sized octopus were sticking on the walls and on the floor.

"This place feels so eerie."

"Yes, it certainly seems to be," replied the professor.

They moved in about fifty meters, before they reached a large space like a den inside that cave. They pointed their lights in all directions, trying to scour the big area in front of them.

"Hey team, can you hear us?" asked Jay over his phone. But there was no response. They were disconnected from the rest of the team on the boat.

Both of them looked around. It was a large space and at one of the corners they saw something. It was some kind of metallic looking structure.

"Professor, look over there. Is that some kind of ship, or some mechanical device?"

"Can't say for sure from this distance. Let us go closer."

They swam further towards that structure.

On getting closer, they could see a large oval-shaped vessel. It was shining when the light touched its surface. Unlike the ship wreckage, it was unaffected by the saline water and the ocean creatures. No algae had grown on the surface. It was a round object of diameter about a fifty feet and height around thirty feet.

Jay and Professor Doherty closed in further and reached near the vessel and touched its surface. With their touch, a few lights started glowing.

"What the hell... is this...?" said Jay. His curiosity was growing like an enormous bubble, yearning to burst anytime.

Discovering an object that was not supposed to be there, the professor was equally surprised.

They were about to go around the object, when suddenly, they heard a noise of rubbing metal come from one of side of that object. A rectangular door of the object was opening up. The door was sliding upwards and revealing the inside of the object. White light was glowing on the inside.

"What shall we do, Professor?"

"Let us go in."

CHAPTER 6

Unidentified Object

Professor reached the door. Jay followed him. Professor swam across the door only to fall suddenly on the ground.

"Argh... what is this?" shouted the Professor. There was no water inside the object and due to gravity Professor Doherty fell down on the floor. Although he fell down just a meter, he hurt himself, as this was unexpected.

Seeing this, Jay was alert, and he stepped in carefully into the door as he went in. He, too, felt the sudden weight because of no water buoyancy, but he was not hurt.

He lent his hand to Professor and helped him get on his feet.

"Professor, this is unbelievable. How can water not enter this space inside this object?" asked Jay.

"There must be sufficient pressure in here to keep the fluid away, but... but...that is not sufficient. There must be something more here," said Professor Doherty, as he got on his feet and supported his waist with his right hand.

Both Jay and Professor Doherty were now inside the unidentified, strange object. They were standing on their feet with air surrounding them instead of water. Water dripping down their skin and suit.

Jay slowly removed his oxygen pipe, wanting to feel the air.

"There is air in here, Professor. I can breathe, and this feels much comfortable and light, as if the oxygen content is much higher than what is outside."

Professor also removed the pipe and felt the oxygen rich air.

He was happy in one corner of his brain, and curious at the other. He knew he had found something unnatural.

One who takes the dive to the bottom gets the pearl. He was saying this to his self.

They were standing in the corridor that was connected to the door through which they entered. They went further in, trying to explore the vessel. The corridor was about a few feet long and it led to a big circular hall.

The wall of the corridor looked black with some shining gem stones embedded on it, that reflected light when it fell on them. Walking slowly, they followed the path from which a white light was emanating.

They entered the hall. Suddenly, a robotic voice shattered the silence.

"Welcome Manu to the Shree Vimana. This is Shree here. Let me know what can I do for you?"

This was completely out of the horizon of human expectation. Surprise took aback both. Now they were also filled with a little fear and thrill.

A cocktail of chemicals rushed in their nerves; such was the mix of their emotions.

They looked around to find the source of the voice. But could not see anyone.

"Who are you?" asked Jay.

"O' Dear Manu, I am the robotic assistant of this ship. My name is Shree."

"Who is Manu? Why are you calling us Manu?" asked Jay, who had many questions in his mind.

"Manu is the designation for the king of humanity. And you are the Manu, my lord," said Shree in her robotic voice.

"Please call me Jay, not Manu... please."

"As you say Sir."

While Jay was talking with Shree, the Professor looked around the hall to find the source of the voice. He moved to the other side of the hall and discovered a stairway going to the next level.

"Hey Jay, come here. The voice seems to be coming from the next level. Let us go there," said the Professor, waving his hand towards Jay.

Jay moved towards Professor Doherty and followed him upstairs.

They went to the top level. At the third level, which was the topmost one, they could see a circular panel containing various buttons and levers.

"This seems to be the control room of this object, Professor."

"Yes, Jay. This looks like a bridge room where the captain of the ship steers the ship from."

"And look over there. That's the front screen through which you can see ahead."

"Wow, so this is a submerged ship," said Jay.

"Shree, where did this ship sail from?" asked Jay.

"This ship has made many voyages. Prior to this, it was at Kushasthali," responded the robotic voice.

"Isn't this Kushasthali the same as Dwarka?" Jay remembered the conversation he had with Swamiji in Ahmedabad.

"Not exactly, Sir. Geographically, they may be the same, but are thousands of years apart."

Momentarily, both Jay and the Professor looked strangely at what the robotic assistant was saying.

"Ok, so it is the old name and new name connection!" exclaimed Jay.

"Yes, kind of," responded Shree.

Jay and Professor went ahead and touched the control panel that had a few red lights blinking and had other button and levers.

With one touch, the ship was lighted all throughout, with white light. Both of them were mesmerised to see that unidentified object from inside. It looked as if they had entered a highly scientifically advanced laboratory.

The transparent window all-round the room was glowing and they could see marine lives outside from that window. On the inside, they could see several screens that were projecting three-dimensional images of planets, sun and galaxies.

"And from where has this come?" asked Jay

"From *Dharaa*."

"And where exactly is *Dharaa?* Is this somewhere in Atlantic or in the Arabian Sea?" he further queried.

"No Jay, Dharaa is not on this planet. It is a planet in Akash-Ganga, the Milky Way Galaxy, but on the other side of the Sun.

"What? Is this some kind of spaceship?" asked Professor, in astonishment.

"That is right, sir. This is the Shree-Vimana," said the robotic voice, Shree.

***

For Jay, the sense of thrill was now getting overturned by the emotion of fear. He was feeling a little uneasy hearing the answers from the voice assistant.

Professor Doherty, on the other hand was excited. He had expected a long-lost city, but he was witnessing now a futuristic ship. He was not able to believe what he was encountering.

In the excitement, he began to push some of the button on the panel. He himself was not sure what he wanted to do. But with the hit of a few buttons and some touch on the screen, the ship started revving.

"Professor, did you start this vehicle?"

"Not that I intended to, but seem like I have."

They felt tremors and then a feeling of weightlessness immersed them from within. Both of them were floating in the air.

"What is happening, Shree?" shouted Jay.

"Sir, you have switched on the Space-Time Portal."

"And... and ... what is that?"

"You would be navigating my memory lanes. And memories are nothing but the projection from the parallel universe. You are being transported in the matrix of space-time. After you are transported, remember to search for this ship in that space-time and only then will you be able to go back."

That was the last thing they heard. And both of them started to revolve- round the control panel in air. They felt as if they were being sucked by a tornado.

Indeed, that was a tornado that connected space-time portals.

Jay and Professor, rolled and twisted by the centrifugal force of the tornado, were going into an unconscious state. They could no longer keep their eyes open and senses awake to the turbulence going around them. They lost their senses, only to feel relieved from the pain they were going through.

The tornado inside the object came to a rest.

CHAPTER 7

KUSHASTHALI

Jay and Professor were lying unconscious on the ground, on the shores of a lake. Jay moved his hands towards his eyes, trying to remove the dirt from his eyelids. He slowly opened his eyes to see a bright daylight.

Where are we? How did we come here? Thought rushed in his head, as he looked around and observed the beautiful garden at the shore of the lake.

He moved his head to get the full glimpse of the place. And then he saw his professor lying on the ground a few feet away. He hastily went up to him and pushed his hand and head.

"Professor... Sir... Are you okay?"

"Can you hear me, sir?" he asked in a frenzy.

"Aahh..." moaned the old man, moving his hand and turning his head.

"Thank god, you are alive," sighed Jay.

"I am feeling exhausted... Uh... Where are we, Jay?" asked the Professor.

"Don't know Sir," replied Jay.

Both got up, looking around in the hope of finding someone who they could talk to. But they could find none. The surrounding was beautiful, but the silence added a sense of eerie to it.

They moved away from the lake shore in search of any habitation. They followed a road that was laid down in that garden.

Going by a few hundred feet, they saw some people besides the road. The people were dressed in a very simple cloth that seemed to be from the medieval age.

"Where are we?" asked Jay again.

Professor responded, "more appropriate question would be - when are we?"

Both of them remembered the last thing they heard from Shree in the unidentified object they had been to.

They went near to the group of people, and said, "Hello, friends, can you help us?"

But to their astonishment, they were unheard. No one responded to them.

Jay moved closer to them and tried to touch one of them. But he could not. His hand moved over the body of the man, as if it was a projected image. Jay could only feel air and no flesh.

Seeing this, the Professor moved his hand as well. He too tried to move one of those men, but could only move some air.

However, they could hear them. These men were speaking in Sanskrit. Jay and the Professor could get a feel with the tone of their voice and some words they could catch.

"Sir, we can see them, we can hear them, but we cannot interact with them. Is this the space-time matrix? Is this the parallel universe?" asked Jay.

"I am also experiencing this first time, my friend," said the professor.

By now, the professor was feeling much better, and there was peace and serenity on his face. He was at a juncture of life when experiencing new and out of world things brought excitement and pleasure rather than fear and anxiety. But for Jay, this experience was unique. He was starting to lose his calm now. He was getting more and more impatient.

Professor noticed that Jay was disturbed. He kept his hand over Jay's shoulder as they moved away from those people, further following the road.

"Jay, you need to be patient. You need to hold on to your nerves. We are in some dimension where no one has come. We need to solve this dimension and get out of this maze. But we can only do this if we have control over our thoughts. Remember, if there is serenity in the soul, the mind can do wonders," Professor Doherty said to Jay while they walked.

They kept walking, following the road. On the way, they could see chariots with horses running down the road, soldiers with spears and swords walking in columns, and citizens busy in their daily chores. It was a mid-day and everyone seemed to be occupied in their work.

Soon they reached the busy city centre. The road was lined with shops on both sides. Men and women were buying and selling the goods, exchanging money that shined like gold. Children dressed in single piece linen and carrying books made of tree barks and leaves were walking on the footpaths.

"What a city this is! So many people but still so much organized. Is this the history we belong to?" asked Jay.

"Everything seems to be in order, my friend. And women are equally participating in the governance of this city. That is called good administration!" exclaimed the professor.

Jay and Professor Doherty continued on their way and came to a roundabout where some soldiers were making some announcement.

"Dear citizens, please pay your valuable attention. Honourable King Kakudmi has announced for the *Swayamvar* of princess Revati. Our beautiful and worthy princess would be selecting a rightful spouse for herself. But this would be determined after a tough challenge that would test the intelligence, strength, power and tactfulness of the candidates. Many kings and princes have received invitations on this occasion. At the same time, citizens are also welcome to participate in this challenge if they feel they can do it...."

Jay and Kakudmi could hardly understand the language but guessed that some kind of ceremony would be organized in the coming days.

They continued their walk further, following the road and taking turns towards the direction where most people were walking. Soon they reached the gates of an enormous palace. This was the King's palace and his office. It was heavily guarded by armoured soldiers. The big gate was closed and there was a small gate just on the right side through which people were passing by one after the other, after being carefully examined by the soldiers and the checking authorities.

"Shall we try snooping through this gate, Professor," asked Jay.

"Oh yes, we are invisible anyway. Let us go to the Palace and see if we get any clue of that object which can send us back to our world," responded Professor Doherty.

"Certainly, sir, that object is the only hope for us. We have to find that, anyhow!"

Both of them stealthily crossed the gate, being non-existent to the people of *that* world. They were in a matrix where they can only see and hear. They couldn't feel anyone, nor could anyone feel them.

They continued walking inside the fortress and reached the palace building. The building glowed as if it were made of gold, or at least had gold plating on its walls. Inside the palace, there was a smooth and furry carpet covering the floor. The sight of the grandeur before them held them in a state of mesmerisation. They kept moving their head observing each object inside the palace hall. The flower vases, decorated tables, walls ornamented with weapons, and the cozy chairs and couches caught their eyes.

"What a grand life the residents of this palace would be living," said an awestruck Jay.

Both of them walked inside, crossing several rooms that were linked with each other. As they passed various rooms, they looked out each and every corner of it in search of the unidentified object, the Shree Vimana, that could send them back to their world. They guessed that such an extraordinary object has to be a government possession, and hence looking for it in a government building was obvious.

In one hall, Professor Doherty moved further towards a grand sized table that had all the fruits beautifully placed on the top, along with shining cutleries. This was the royal dining table placed at the centre of the hall.

"Are you hungry, Professor?" asked Jay, as he saw the professor getting close to the dining table.

"No, no, Jay. I do not feel like eating. I am just wondering if we have ceased out of hunger by any chance?"

Professor was wondering as feeling of hunger was also a sensory response of the body and they had ceased to experience quite some feelings in this space-time matrix.

"Oh, you are right. I am also beginning to feel the same. Neither we can touch these fruits nor we feel like eating."

A new revelation struck them. They kept on assimilating all the new experiences in the hope of solving the maze. They kept walking and came to a crowded room. This was the Royal Hall, the courtroom of the King.

Seated at the far end of the hall on top of the throne was a huge man with a big beard and big eyes having a golden crown on his head. He was speaking in a loud and clear voice and all others in the room were attentively listening to him. Some of the men and women were seated, whereas some were standing on the sides. Soldiers were guarding the room at the entrances.

As they entered the king's courtroom from the backdoor, the door that connected the room to the Royal Palace, King moved his head towards them. King then looked in their eyes. This was the first time someone had looked at them in the space-time matrix.

King looked at them before moving his head back to the courtroom crowd and continued his speech.

Jay and Professor Doherty looked at each other. They were facing another surprising moment. Neither said anything, but both had a lot to speak.

King, meanwhile, was making an announcement.

"In this kingdom of Kushasthali, I pledge that no citizen of this land will sleep without having a meal."

CHAPTER 8

VIBRATIONS

The court closed, and the crowd was dismissed. King rose and stood on his feet. As he stepped down from the golden throne, his heavy strides were making a loud sound with each step. He was a tall man, more than eight feet. He looked strong and muscular. Not only him, but all the people, including the citizens, were of great height. Everyone crossed the seven feet mark.

Jay and Professor Doherty looked at the tall king as he walked down and proceeded to his palace. They chased the king. The soldiers escorted King for half his way until he entered his personal room.

In his personal room, he was followed by no one else but the two matrix walkers, Jay and Dr Doherty.

As the king approached the middle of the room, he turned back and looked at both of them.

He said, "Who are you, dear friends, and from where have you come?"

Jay was awestruck. So was the Professor, but he kept his awe within himself and responded, "Can you see us?"

"No, but I can feel you. I can feel your vibrations," replied Kakudmi.

"But how can you do so when no one else can see and feel us? Are you also a matrix-walker?" asked the professor again.

"No, I am not. I am just another resident on this planet. But I possess the knowledge and sense to catch vibrations from other dimensions," said Kakudmi.

He paused for a while and then continued, "this is all about vibrations. With mantras, we achieve the state where we can catch frequencies from other worlds, be it in human, spirits, divine or several other dimensions. I know your vibrations are not from this human world, but I can feel your presence. I can even feel the vibration of each of your senses. So, in a way, I have the image of yours in front of me."

Kakudmi was a great king. Having traced the footsteps of his ancestors, he had charted his own course. He was a descendant of Vaivasvat Manu and he had inherited the art of administration, and leadership. He, thus, had done very well as a King. However, his learning was not only limited to the kingship, but he also had the honour to learn from the great *Saptarishi*. He was a regular visitor to *Rishi-Ashrams*and never missed any opportunity to provide his services to them. As a result, he had learnt many scientific and spiritual techniques from them. He also took to austerity while serving his duties as a king and achieved many *siddhis*. It was because of these siddhis, under the guidance of Rishis, that he had attained this power to communicate with beings from other dimensions.

"And how can you speak our language, sir?" asked Jay.

"Language is just a medium. Even you are not using your tongue. We all are using our cerebral senses to connect to one another and communicate via these senses. This is telepathy," responded the king.

This was another revelation. Both Jay and Professor Doherty realized that indeed they were not using their tongues all this while they were talking to each other.

"But if that is the case, why were we not able to understand other citizens' speech out there in the city?" Jay cross questioned.

"Because they were not transmitting via vibrations. They were speaking their normal language."

"Now, you tell me - who are you both?" asked Kakudmi.

"Sir, we have come from another dimension and in that dimension, we are from the *future* of your *time*. We are not from this time. We are stuck in the space-time matrix because of one unidentified object named Shree."

"Ha ha ha," King Kakudmi laughed out loud. "I understand now. So, you now belong to neither world - not this, not the other one. You are hanging in between."

Seeing the king laugh, Jay felt at ease. He now had someone who knew their misery. And a ray of hope was beginning to pierce through the darkness.

"O' dear king, we are looking out for that object that can send us back to the space-time where we belong. Can you help us find that object?" asked Professor Doherty.

On hearing about their need for Shree Vimana, the King went silent. He was thinking something deep in his head and so was visible on his face. After a while, he spoke.

"Hmm, I see. I have that object in my possession. But I cannot give that to you now. You shall get that when the time comes. Until then, you both are my royal guests. Make yourself comfortable in this palace. You can put up in this very room where you are now," said Kakudmi as he moved out of that room.

Jay and the Professor had a mix of emotions. On one side, they saw hope. And on the other side, they started seeing a delay in their transfer. Both of them sat on the couch of the room looking around and thinking about their next move.

***

King Kakudmi, engrossed in his thought, moved to his daughter's room. He had been looking for a right match for her daughter for some time now. He knew that his daughter is one of the most brilliant minds the world had. No one could match her intelligence and wit. She was also an accomplished writer and singer and a gallant warrior of the era. Many a time, when the King himself ran out of ideas and did not find a solution to a problem, he rushed to his daughter for her advice.

Revati was reading some palm manuscripts in her room. She was back from her daily armoury practice and was doing some reading and writing.

Looking at the king, Revati stood up. She stood at the same height as her father. She was a beautiful lady and confidence exuberated from her face.

"What is troubling you, dear father?" asked Revati.

"My dear daughter, you know I have planned the *Swayamvar* for tomorrow. But I am very sceptical if we could find the right man," said Kakudmi.

"You know it is so difficult to find a man who is both a sharp soldier and a brilliant mind," he further added.

"Don't you worry, father. I am in no hurry to find a husband."

"But you know I do not have much time left with me and for the remainder of my life, I would like to retire and live a life of penance. Moreover, I have no other descendant who can care for this state and the people," responded Kakudmi.

"O' dear father, let me tell you one story," said Revati and she continued, "long back there lived a king. He had two daughters. As the king grew older, the worry of who would rule his kingdom grieved him. The king would spend sleepless nights just thinking about what he should do to find the right matches for his daughters. Both the daughters knew their father's reason for sadness, but they were not suitable to perform their father's duties as a king. That was the time of previous *Kaliyug* and daughters did not rule the state. And so, they could not help their father, even if they wished to do so."

"One fine day, a sage arrived in the king's palace. The king and the two princesses served the old sage with dedication and devotion. Sage was happy to receive such a good hospitality, and he said the two princesses to ask for a boon from him. The two princesses asked for brave and gallant husbands who could prove to be the heir of their father," said Revati as the king was listening intently.

She further continued, "the sage gave the blessing for their wishes to be true. The very next day, the elder princess met a prince of another kingdom who had come to their city. Both fell in love. During same time, the younger daughter met with a brave soldier from her own kingdom and they also fell in love. In a few days, the marriage ceremonies were performed, and both lived a happy married life, until one day when the king called upon both the couples to discuss his will."

"King wanted to give away his kingdom to the younger daughter and her spouse because he believed that his younger son-in-law belonged to same kingdom and hence would take care of the kingdom better. But this did not go down well with the elder son-in-law. He raised his claim as he was the elder one. And so, there started a fight. The fight went on to become bloody. Both sons-in-law, accompanied by their men, killed each other. After all, they both were gallant and brave and right heirs of the kingdom, as per the blessing from the sage."

Revati stopped and asked her father, "now, dear father, tell me what is the use of such blessings and such husbands, if fate has something else written for them?"

King had understood his daughter's story. He said, "you are right Revati. Nothing can happen more than the fate, and earlier than the time."

CHAPTER 9

SWAYAMVAR

King's throne-hall was decorated with flowers and jewels. The band people were playing melodious tunes to soothe the ears of the kings, queens, princes and the citizens who were invited to the royal ceremony of Swayamvar. The pomp and grandeur of the royal hall was evident of the prosperity the kingdom had.

King had not left anything that would have made the ceremony look grander. After all, he was going to choose the right match for his only daughter, and the probable heir to the throne.

The hall was packed with people. Everyone seated on the comfortable and cozy seats allocated to them. The hall also had an audience who were not participants. King had invited all the respectable people of the society and the Rishis to seek their blessings.

"Let the proceedings begin," announced the King, and he nodded towards Suketu, his minister and spokesman of the courtroom.

Suketu stood up to explain the rules of the game.

He announced, "Dear friends, thank you for being here at this historical event. I must now explain all the rules of this *Swayamvar*. To marry our beautiful princess, one must have to pass two steps."

Suketu then paused for a moment before delving into the details. He said further, pointing his index finger towards the centre of the ceiling, "As you can see, this chandelier decorated with flowers, instead of lamps. You can see many types of flowers in there. But there is one lotus at the centre of it. To be successful in this stage, you need to use your bow and arrow to bring down that lotus. But you should do that without breaking the chandelier and without dropping any of the other flowers."

"Holy cow, this is impossible," murmured the old professor.

Professor and Jay were also seeing this magnanimous event from one corner of the hall.

"This is insane, sir. No one can do this," said Jay in response.

Suketu continued, "And that is the stage one. One who passes this stage needs to answer a question from the princess. If he answers that correctly, he would be the righteous match for the princess."

With the announcement of the rules, the hall went silent. All the participant gazing at one another to see who attempts first.

The spectators saw the proceedings curiously and delightfully.

After a few minutes, a prince stood up. He pulled out his bow and arrow from his side and walked to the platform that was created for the participants to stand and aim for the flower.

Aiming towards the flower, he stretched the strings of the bow, murmured a few verses, and set the arrow free. The arrow missed the target.

One after the other, each participant tried their skill and luck. But no one could succeed until a young man in ordinary clothes representative of a common citizen stepped in.

He aimed and perfectly hit the target. His arrow could dislodge the lotus from its position and the flower fell down on the ground.

Everyone was enthralled by his talent. The crowd burst out in jubilation. King looked quite happy. After all, someone from his kingdom has done what no one else could do.

He was called up near the King's throne.

"What is your name, dear friend?" asked Suketu.

"I am Kalyan, a herder by profession, but an archer by passion. I look after the cattle and sell dairy products for living. In my spare time, I train myself in warrior skills," responded the young man.

"Very well, Kalyan. Now you would have to answer a question from our princess."

Suketu then directed him to walk near the princess.

Princess stood up and said, "O' great archer, can you tell what is God's food? What does he eat?"

Perplexity filled Kalyan as he had anticipated a question of general awareness or something related to social and moral sciences, but he did not expect anything like this.

He thought for some time. But his mind was blank. And it was visible on his face.

After thinking for some more time, he said, "O' my princess, I do not have an answer. All I have seen are the fruits and sweets offered to gods. So, my thought is only limited to that. But I am sure your question pervades many layers of philosophy and cannot be this simple. Please accept my apologies."

Princess applauded Kalyan's honesty and praised him for his skill and his thoughts.

King Kakudmi felt disheartened by the contestant's failure, but he also felt flattered by the honesty of the common man. He said, "dear Kalyan, although you could not be successful in this Swayamvar, you are a great archer and I offer you a position in my army."

Kalyan was happy that he managed to impress the King with his armoury skill and also secure a job for himself.

"Thank you, O' King. But I would also like to know the answer to this question from Princess," said Kalyan.

King nodded, looking at the princess.

Princess Revati said, "the answer to this is 'false pride', *ahamkaar*. God eats false pride whenever human beings take undue pride and become excessive egoist. God comes down to eat that *ahamkaar*."

Hearing the answer, the hall was filled with applause and praises.

After some more participants, the Swayamvar ended without any success. King was sad. Yet again he was not successful in his endeavour of finding a rightful match for Revati. He left for his room, followed by his daughter. All the king's men also departed, leaving behind the two souls from different dimension.

"I told you, no one can do such a stunt," said Professor Doherty.

"But one of them did that, sir, although he could not pass the second round," responded Jay.

"If the king wants to marry his daughter, he must have to lower his expectations and should let us depart from here," murmured the professor.

***

King Kakudmi, Revati and Suketu walked to the King's room. All of them shared sadness, but it was more visible on the King's face. Revati, although disheartened, was still hopeful. Suketu was finding words to console his king.

"I have tried all that I could, still I am not able to fulfil my fatherly duties, my daughter," said Kakudmi.

"Father, you are doing the best you could. It is not your fault. As I said earlier, nothing can be achieved if its time has not arrived. We all can perform our *dharma*. Getting fruit is not in our hands. So, do not blame yourself."

Hearing words of courage and hope from his daughter was no less comforting than a divine medicine for the king.

Suketu, a very senior member of the kingdom and one who shared a friendly relationship with the king, was in a deep thought. Many things were going on in his mind as he was finding the right words to convey his idea.

"O dear King, the almighty pre-decides the match for everyone in this world. And it is true for the princess as well. So, if this world does not have her match, is he somewhere in other worlds?" asked Suketu.

"What do you want to say, Suketu? Please say it more candidly."

"Sir, as you know, there are many worlds like our earth. There is Dev-Lok, Brahma-Lok, Vaikuntha and many other worlds created by *Para-Amba*, Devi Shakti and run by Shree Vishnu. So, there is a possibility that Revati's husband belongs to one of these worlds."

"Hmm.. yes, that can be. But how can we know for sure?" asked the King.

"Why don't we ask this to all knowledgeable Brahma-Dev? We have the Shree Vimana given by your ancestors that can take you there," suggested Suketu.

King Kakudmi found himself transported back in his memory lanes upon hearing the suggestion from his minister. He thought about his meeting with his ancestor, Vaivasvat Manu, for a moment and said, "I have that in my mind, my friend. I still remember the day when my great ancestor handed me over the Vimana to take care of it and had asked me to use it only when no other option was available to solve the problem."

Kakudmi continued, "I am just weighing the stakes and seeing whether I should use it or not."

He paused for a moment and continued, "you know, Suketu, I am at the crossroads now, trying to figure out which way should I go. One way takes me to using the Vimana and fulfil fatherly duties, thereby allowing me to take *Sanyas* and live the remaining life of a hermit."

He further said, "the other road takes me to a place where I cannot pardon myself for not doing my fatherly duties or compromising with the duties I owe. But then on that road, I would save the *misuse* of the divine Vimana."

Suketu concurred with the king. He understood the dilemma the king was going through. But he wanted to give the best suggestion he could.

Suketu thought for a while and then responded, "dear king, the use, mis-use or abuse would depend on the purpose and the intention. If you are true to your dharma, you would never misuse or abuse the boon and blessings."

"Thank you, Suketu. I understand what you want to say. But I need some time to think before I call upon the services of Shree-Vimana."

Revati was listening to the conversation. She was a wise and intelligent woman. She would give her suggestion only when she was asked. Else, she saved her wisdom to herself.

After the brief conversation, Suketu and Revati dispersed out of the room.

CHAPTER 10

THE INCIDENT

Two days had passed by after the Swayamvar. The daily chores of the kingdom were running as usual. King was busy in performing his duties. The monsoon rains had started and King's men were busy helping out farmers in the upcoming plantation season. It was the duty of the kingdom to provide for the healthy seeds and manures for the agriculture.

Revati, being responsible office bearer and the princess, helped the citizens in all things in her capacity. She was seen as a motherly figure by the citizens. Often, she was called by the name '*Rajkumari Maa*' or sometimes '*Maa Prakriti*'; she was as caring as the mother nature.

Revati was out in the city with her friends and helpers. She was invited as a royal guest to attend the function that was celebrated as the arrival of the rainy season. The citizens performed Shiv puja and planned a feast. Her entourage arrived at the gates of the city hall when they were greeted with garlands and perfume sprays. It was a customary ritual to offer flowers and perfumes to the guests. And she was a special one.

As she entered the hall, Revati could see people were rejoicing the festival. Everyone wore their best attire. Children were busy playing around and had sweets and fruits in their hand. Smiles and laughter were everywhere.

However, to her surprise, she saw an old couple who did not have any happiness on their face. Their eyes were wet. They were looking to reach out to the princess and speak to her, but were hesitant to do so. Revati could read their face, but held her calm and continued to the idol room, the *garbh-griha* of the temple room to perform the puja.

Revati completed the puja as per all the *Sanatan Dharma* rituals and came out looking for the old couple. They were still standing in the same place. Revati walked up to them and asked, "Namaskar, do you want to say anything to me?"

As the princess spoke to them, they folded their hands in respect and tears rolled down their eyes. It was like those drops were waiting for a push.

The old man then spoke, "O mother princess, we seek justice. We had a daughter. We loved her more than our own lives. Last year, we married her to a rich trader. We wanted to give her all the happiness in life. But..."

The old man sobbed and then continued, "the man to whom we married our daughter turned out to be a fraud. He demanded money from us and took away all our belongings. And now, our daughter is no more. He says she was diseased, but we doubt she was killed."

"Now she is gone, and we old souls waiting to depart this earth without any justice."

Revati felt the pain they were going through. She extended her hand and touched the folded palms of the old man, and said, "I would definitely help you. And I promise that justice shall be served. No culprit in my kingdom can escape."

Hearing this coming directly from the most trusted person in the kingdom was akin to hearing god's voice. The old couple showered more tears.

The old women then said, "we loved our daughter more than our lives. Who wouldn't? After all, she was the reason for our laughter, our prayer, and our breath. We wanted to give her all happiness. And now…"

She could not complete her sentence. Emotions choked her throat. She could not speak anymore.

Revati looked towards one of the ministers who accompanied her and said, "Sumant ji, give them all help so that we can at least give them a comfortable life, and take all the required information from them to initiate the case on the culprit."

Sumant took a note of this in his notebook and accompanied the old couple to their home. He was a responsible office bearer, and he made all the arrangements, as asked by the princess. He also lodged a complaint against their son-in-law and initiated a case in the courtroom.

Revati received assurance that someone would take care of things. However, this incident left a mark on her heart. She could feel the pain that only a parent can endure. She realized how important it is for a parent to see their offspring doing well. This was the first time she felt what her father would be feeling for her. She realized how different it is to feel than to understand the feeling.

***

Professor Doherty and Jay were roaming all around in the Royal Palace in search of their *machine*.

"Where the hell is this Vimana?" babbled Professor.

"We have searched every room of this palace, but could not see that. The only place that remains is the underground basement. I have seen the King going in the stairs beneath the carpet of his room," said

Jay.

"Very well, let us go there," responded Professor Doherty.

"We cannot. That place is locked, and the key resides in the thread worn by the King himself. He is guarding that room himself. I am very sure that Vimana should be in there."

"So, what shall we do?"

"King Kakudmi takes out his thread from his body only once during the whole day. And that is during the time he bathes himself. Before he goes to the royal bathroom, he places his thread containing beads and the keys in a box on the table in his room. It is during this short time that key is separated from the King," said Jay with some hope in his eyes.

"Okay then, why to wait longer? Let us be a thief as soon as possible."

"Yes sir, let us do this tomorrow morning."

***

On returning from the celebration, Revati was sad. She had lost the peace in her heart. She didn't waste even a second and went on to see her father. Seeing her father, she embraced him and broke down. She could feel the warmth and comfort in her father's arms.

"What happened, my darling?" said the King.

Revati couldn't stop herself from telling the short story she came across in the annual plantation festival.

"I can feel your pain and concern, dear father. I can understand what would be going within you. You have raised me as a single parent after mother left us for heavenly abode."

"No, no, do not cry, my daughter. You are not supposed to feel the pain now. It is my pain as of now. And it is my responsibility to give you the best you deserve."

"Father, may I ask you to seek help from Shree Vimana now?"

This was the first time Revati was tendering her suggestion unsolicited and also the first time she was asking her father to use the Vimana that was lying dead somewhere. King was surprised hearing his daughter's request, but he, in a way, was looking for this suggestion. Deep in his heart, he wanted a push so that he could use that machine.

"Okay dear Revati, so be it. We shall go to the Brahma Lok and seek Lord Brahma's guidance. I am sure all our sorrows would end and our search would result in fruits."

He further added, "now please get some rest; the day has been a tiring one for you."

CHAPTER 11

SHREE VIMANA

The next morning, Jay and Professor Doherty had all the hopes and fear within. They were foreseeing their freedom back to their dimension, and at the same time they were going to do something they had never done.

Both moved surreptitiously to King's room after ensuring the King would have moved for the bath. They came closer to the table where King had kept the box containing the key.

Jay stretched his hand to grab the box. But to his surprise and later realization, he could not catch it.

"Oh, my god! How could we miss this?" frustrated Jay yelled.

Seeing this, Professor Doherty also realized, "yes, we should have realized this; we cannot touch any of the things of this world."

Disappointed, both of them sat down on the chairs.

"We should think something else. This is not working," said Jay.

"Let us talk with the King."

***

Few minutes later, King Kakudmi came out of the bathroom. And he immediately sensed the presence of the two dimension-walkers.

"What brings you here, my friends?" asked the king.

"O' King, we need to escape this maze. We can only do this with your help. Without you, we are stuck in here," said the Professor.

"I told you, when it is the right time, you shall have the Vimana," said the king.

"We remember that, O' dear lord. What makes us worry is that we might be missing many years back in our time. And it may happen that a single moment in this time frame may cost us years in our original frame," explained the professor.

King Kakudmi had something to think about now. He had not imagined this scenario. Being an empathetic person, he was beginning to worry about the two *ghosts*.

One action of mine can change the future. One help can save two unborn.

Being a good and kind human being, the king thought upon and responded, "okay, I shall take both of you to the Vimana. Let us talk to Shree and see how can we help you. I must also let you know that I would be going for an interstellar travel using that ship by tomorrow. If in the meantime we can help you, we shall not resist in doing so."

King Kakudmi then asked both of them to follow him in to the basement, where he had hidden the *alien* craft.

***

As they stepped in to the stairs leading to underground obscure room, King Kakudmi went on lighting the lamp. Jay and the professor entered the room to find that it was no small room, rather an enormous hall. In the centre was a risen platform that had the object they had seen before.

King Kakudmi pointed towards the object and said, "this is Shree Vimana." He further added, "my ancestor, the Manu of this manvantar, gave me this Vimana. This is no ordinary Vimana; it is also not of this planet. It comes from the planet where humans lived prior to moving to Prithvi, and after that planet was destroyed."

"So, you mean humans have migrated from another planet and not evolved from the monkeys?" asked Jay, astonishingly as this was not lining up with the education he had received.

"Oh yes, we only share our traits with the monkeys, but we are not evolved from them. Rather, we both have been developed by the same life-material and hence we have similar biological traits," responded the king.

King walked up the steps and entered the Vimana. The two matrix-walkers followed him. Jay and the Professor were delighted to see the same Vimana they had used under-sea.

"Wow, it is the same machine," elated Jay spoke.

"Shree?" called Kakudmi.

"Namaste, my King," said Shree and continued, "Please tell me what can I do."

"Shree, these are my friends from a different dimension, who happened to come to this dimension and they say that they used this Vimana to travel across dimensions," answered the King.

"I do not have this in my memory. Moreover, I cannot see anyone other than you here, although I can sense the presence of more souls here."

"You are right. They have interacted with you in the future, so it is logical that you would not have them in your memory. But we need to help them send back to the dimension they belong. And we can do that only when you open the portal for that."

"O dear King, I am running short of fuel. You know this Vimana is fuelled by Amrit. There is no Amrit left in the world. And with the stock that I have here, I am afraid we cannot do cross-dimensional transit."

This was a shock for Jay and Professor Doherty. This was their only hope and now they are facing the challenge of fuel shortage.

Is this the end of the road? Can't we get back to our time ever?

The thoughts sped up to their mind like lightning speed. Hope was being eclipsed by scepticism.

Hearing this, the King felt equally devastated. Although his reason was different.

King said, "Hey Shree, I need to make an important travel, and this is the question of my life and death. I have plans to travel to Brahma Lok with my daughter Revati. And your revelation about fuel is worrying me. How can we now travel to see Lord Brahma?"

"Dear King, that we can certainly do. We have enough of Amrit in reserve to travel to anywhere in this dimension and so we can travel to Brahma Lok and get back," said Shree.

Hearing this King took a breath of relief. His hopes were still alive.

King moved his head towards Jay and Professor, "my friends, you hear Shree? Although we would like to help you, we cannot."

Jay had something on his mind. He was thinking out and then said to the King, "Sir, can we at least send out a message in the future to ourselves stating the story so that we never come to this place?"

"Let us ask Shree."

"Shree, you would have sensed this man's thought. Is there any way we can do this?"

"Yes Sir, I can send out a message to their dimension but that too would be at the expense of fuel. So, allow me to send as much of the message as we can after reserving the fuel for the return trip to Brahma Lok," said Shree.

"Very well, that makes sense."

"Friends, you can tell Shree what message and mode of communication you would want to send."

Jay was happy a little at hearing this. He said to Shree, "Hey Shree, please send this message via email to doherty at nyuniversity dot edu - *Professor, do not go on this mission. If you go to this mission, you would be trapped in another dimension, and you would not be able to return. I am sending this message from that dimension in the past. Never venture on this mission. I request again. Jay."*

Shree noted every word and prepared a message to be sent to the mailbox in another dimension. In a few moments she replied, "message sent successfully, but I could only send the first seven words in the message as sending more was not viable, given that I have to save fuel."

"Oh my god, so only message that was sent is - *Professor, do not go on this mission"*

Professor, meanwhile, was connecting the dots. He realized it was exactly the same message he had received prior to the start of the mission.

"Let us go Jay and Doherty. We need to think of another solution for this problem. I am sure we could find a way out. Meanwhile, I would also travel to Brahma Lok and by the time I am back, we can figure out a way," said the King before coming out of the Vimana.

CHAPTER 12

THE JOURNEY

King, Revati and Suketu were in the room, having discussion on the matters of the kingdom. King explained all that happened in the Shree Vimana and about the two people from the future. Revati and Suketu were awestruck. They never had thought such a thing as dimension travel could exist.

King said, "we will handle that problem, but as of now, I want all of us to focus on our travel to Brahma Lok."

He added, "Suketu, you know very well how important it is to me to fulfil my fatherly duties. Without which my *dharma* would not be protected. And I shall always be in debt to this world. I have no way now, other than to seek advice from the Brahma Dev himself."

Suketu understood the king's decision and was worried as to how the kingdom would run in the absence of both, the King and the princess.

"How long will you be gone, O King?" "And who shall be the caretaker of the throne?" asked Suketu.

"What I have understood from my *Pitridev*, Manu, is that it takes one lunar cycle to reach Brahma-Lok and another one to return, using the Shree Vimana. So, we shall be back in slightly more than 2 months, given that we may stay there for some moments," replied the King.

"Father, if I am not wrong, the time in Brahma Lok runs at a different speed than on Earth. So, a few moments in Brahma Lok would cost us a few days on Earth, and so we cannot afford to stay much longer in there," said Revati. She was a knowledgeable woman and knew about the time-dilation science by reading religious texts and talking to the Saptarishi.

"You are right, my dear, and that is why I have added a few more days to the estimated two months," replied the King before turning his head towards Suketu.

He continued, "Dear friend, Suketu, coming to your second question, I feel that no one other than you is the right person to guard the throne. Under your command, we have protected our borders from many attacks. You also know which lever to pull to make things happen. I would designate you as the right protector of the throne."

Suketu was happy to confirm once again that he was the most trusted person for the King. At the same time, he was feeling the weight of responsibilities on his shoulders. He knew what to do in known situations. What was worrying him was how to handle the unknowns.

"Please also make the preparations for our travel, Suketu. We would be leaving tomorrow afternoon," instructed Kakudmi.

King Kakudmi waited for a moment to see if Suketu has any doubts or concern. Upon no response from him, he continued, "and one more thing, Suketu. That young man, Kalyan. Give him all the trainings. He has the capability of becoming an excellent commander for our army."

Kalyan was the young man who had crossed the first stage of Swayamvar but had failed in the second stage.

"As you say, my king."

***

The fateful day arrived. All the arrangements for the royal

departure were done. King called a meeting of his ministers and announced his travel plan. He also designated Suketu as the caretaker in the absence of the royal linage. Suketu humbly followed the orders and so did other members of the ministry.

Post this meeting, Kakudmi and Revati moved to the basement along with the supplies that would be required for their travel. Both of them entered the Shree Vimana.

This was the first time Revati had got into the *alien* craft.

While both of them were busy setting up their gears, the air of Jay and Professor Doherty also boarded the craft. However, it was not long that King could sense their presence.

"What are you both doing here?" asked the King, without speaking any word.

"Dear King, we would like to accompany you. We never know where would this craft go and whether we will see this again. Please accommodate us as well. We would not participate in any of your meetings or would not interfere in your work," said Jay. His communication reflected a sense of mercy and that melted King's heart.

"Okay, fine. Just be in this craft. Do not off board this Vimana even when we disembark it."

"We swear. We shall be here and remain here until you ask us to go out," said Professor Doherty.

King nodded and moved to the bridge of the spaceship.

"Hey Shree," said Kakudmi.

"Yes, Sir. Please tell me what can I do for you."

"Let us set off to the Brahma Lok, following the co-ordinates as fed by Vaivasvat Manu."

"Sure, sir, I see two passengers aboard this ship. Please, both of you, make yourself comfortably seated and seatbelts fastened. The two of the spirits are free to hover along with me," instructed the robotic voice.

King and Revati followed the instruction. Meanwhile, Shree announced the closure of the Vimana's door and opening of the pathway inside the basement that led to the open ground in the Palace's backyard.

"Dear King and Princess, we are taking off now," said Shree.

With that, they felt a momentary zero gravity and the Vimana slowly hovered and floated swiftly to come out of the underground basement. The Vimana then sped up with great acceleration. Before long, King and Revati could see clouds surrounding the windows of the Vimana. In the next few moments, they could witness darkness being painted outside the window. The Vimana had now reached the outer space.

"We are now out of earth's atmosphere and soon would also be out of its gravitational realm. You all can remove your seatbelts and feel at comfort. The gravity and air pressure inside this ship has been calibrated to make you feel earth-like," Shree announced and that brought a little smile on Revati's face, who was making air and space travel for the first time in her life. King Kakudmi was also not a frequent flier, but at least he had travelled once in the past as a company to Vaivasvat Manu.

The Shree Vimana had taken this trip earlier, and hence had all the co-ordinates and manoeuvres in its memory. It required no captain to pilot it.

Revati and Kakudmi, upon getting freed up from the seatbelts, moved close to the window screen overlooking the vast expanse of the dark space. The sight of celestial objects glowing from the sun's rays mesmerized them.

Revati was enchanted by this experience. She said, looking towards her father, "thank you father for taking up this journey. I had only imagined how planets and moon can look, and now we can see it so vividly."

***

For the next thirty days, the father and the daughter duo kept themselves busy in reading, cooking, exercising and watching the stars and galaxies outside of the ship. Often, they would feel tired and sick of the dark space, but also rejoiced the moments when they witnessed the spectacle of galactic objects.

"What a great journey this has been, dear father. Leave aside what we would gain from the consultation with Lord Brahma, and this trip and these spectacles are in itself a heavenly experience," said Revati as they looked on to a comet that was flying by a nearby star.

"Very few people in the history of humanity have achieved the feat of coming out of the realm of Bhu-Lok, the world of humans. It is our good karma that has earned this honour and trust of Manu. It is because of him that we are taking the services of this great out-of-the-world Vimana," responded Kakudmi. He had a sense of pride when he spoke.

There was a momentary silence, and it was broken by the robotic voice of Shree.

"Dear passengers, please be seated and seat belts fastened. We are now attempting the entry into the Brahma Lok's atmosphere. There would be a jerk, but we would stabilize it very soon. As a precautionary measure, please sit tight."

Revati and Kakudmi followed the instruction.

From the window shield, they could see the bright light. The brightness kept on increasing, and then a spectrum of dispersed light formed on the windowpane. They felt a little deceleration, but in the next moment, they were at ease.

The craft was floating in the air of the planet. It hovered over as it came closer to the ground. Revati could see the lush green lawn outside.

"This is the port of Brahma Lok where all the alien ships land. We would be off boarding the Vimana here and would be escorted on this planet's vehicles on to the Lord Brahma's chambers," said Kakudmi. He had heard stories from the Manu about the visits and, hence, he had an idea of all the procedures in the Brahma Lok.

CHAPTER 13

BRAHMA-LOK

"I hope you both remember what you promised," said Kakudmi, looking towards the bridge.

"Yes, dear King, we remember very well. You be assured we are not going to leave this ship," responded Jay while the Professor nodded in confirmation. Professor, although was not thinking to break the promise, he was thinking what all can be done while being inside the ship.

"And do not worry, once we are back, we shall look how to solve your problem and send you back home," assured the King before moving out of the craft, holding his daughter's hand.

The moment they stepped out of the craft and put their feet on the lawn, a vehicle drew closer to them, hovering in the air and drifting close to the ground. The vehicle, shaped like a car, landed next to Revati and its door opened up. A robotic voice echoed from inside the car, "please be seated King Kakudmi and Princess Revati. You are welcome in this world."

Revati and Kakudmi followed what the robotic assistant instructed. They adjusted themselves inside the car. The car closed its door before drifting in the air at a great speed.

"You can call me Bani, King Kakudmi. While you are here on this planet, I shall be your ride assistant," said the robotic voice.

"Thank you, Bani," responded Kakudmi.

Flying over the marvellous city that was a confluence of the nature at its best and the technology at its apex. It had high-rise buildings glowing with neon lights amidst green forests, waterfalls, mountains, and river in the surrounding. The space was not very busy; very few flying vehicles were hovering and drifting.

"This is a God's abode in genuine sense," said Revati.

The look of the advanced city fascinated her. She came from a world where night lights were only oil lamps and moonlight. In this world she was sighting the electricity powered lamps and glowing signboards. Everything from the flying *chariots* to tall buildings and robotic assistant was enough to enchant her.

In the next few minutes, they reached their destination as the car landed on the lawn outside of the Grand Palace of Lord Brahma. Revati and Kakudmi alighted the car and moved inside the Palace.

***

Revati and Kakudmi felt very light while walking on the lawn. The gravity was lesser than on Earth and this made them feel light. A slight push, and they jumped several feet away. Upon realization, they maintained the push and pace to make themselves comfortable with the new environment and the new world.

They walked past the main entrance, only to be greeted by a gatekeeper. He looked alien, with big eyes popping out of his triangular face and a bald head. He was thin but tall, much higher than the earth-dwellers.

"Namaste. You are welcome here, King Kakudmi and Princess Revati," he said with seemingly a smile on his face.

"Namaste, my dear friend," said the king and continued, "we are here to meet Brahma Dev and seek his blessings. May you please guide us? Where shall we go to meet him?"

"We know about it, dear king. Why don't you make yourself

comfortable in the guest room? Brahma Dev is busy with the *Yakshas* right now. He shall be with you pretty soon," he said, signalling them to follow him.

All three of them walked to a room just next to the Brahma's court. In the courtroom, Brahma Dev was presiding over a meeting. They could hear some voices coming out of the courtroom but could not understand, as if it was an alien language. While they passed the rooms of the Royal Palace, Revati and Kakudmi could see beings other than humans passing by. Some looked like earthly-animals others looked like hybrids of humanoids and animals.

"They remind me of *Daksha Prajapati* and *Shree Ganesh*, father," murmured Revati. The legends of Daksha Prajapati having head of a goat and Shree Ganesh having head of elephant were running through their head as they saw such beings in the Brahma Lok.

"Yes, I am also thinking about them. Either they are surgically modified or maybe they are born this way," responded Kakudmi.

As they reached the room having couch and tables, the gatekeeper who was escorting them stopped and said, "please make yourselves comfortable here. Do not be worried about the strange-looking beings. All of them are eminent scholars and Rishis who are here because of their *dharma*."

Brahma Lok and its residents were no ordinary beings either; they were the master of the Yog and garnered the yogic energy to feel other's minds and soul. Hence, what was going on in their minds was not hidden from the gatekeeper.

"Thank you, Sir for those clarifying words. I know this place is the abode of the lord. Everyone here has to be *dharmic*," said

Kakudmi as they sat down on the cushioned chairs.

Revati then asked the gatekeeper, "dear sir, how long shall we be waiting to get a visit of the lord?"

"Mam, it is difficult to say, but you can expect in about half a *muhurta.*"

Muhurta is a unit of time and measures approximately 48 minutes on the earth. Half muhurta equals about 24 minutes.

Revati and Kakudmi were a little uncomfortable hearing this. They looked at each other. They knew that time on Brahma Lok runs at a slower pace and hence, few minutes would be a much longer time on earth. What they were not aware of was how much longer that dilation would be. So, they were taken aback by hearing this, but unfortunately, they had no other option. They had to visit the lord whatever it takes.

***

The wait was exactly half a muhurta, as suggested by the gatekeeper, but it seemed like a century for them. However, time never stalls. And there is always an end to a wait.

The door of the courtroom opened and all the Yakshas, gods and court-men and women came out of the court. One of the men from them walked to Revati and Kakudmi and informed that Brahma wanted to see them.

This was news of delight for the king and the princess. Without losing even a single moment, they rushed to the courtroom where Brahma was seated on the lotus throne.

"Om Brahmane Namaha," said Revati and Kakudmi with folded hands, as they entered and stood in front of the lotus throne.

"Kalyanam, O king and princess," said Brahma.

He further added, "tell me King Kakudmi, what brings you here?"

"O dear lord. My fatherly duties are unfinished, and this is stalling my progress in the path of dharma. I seek your blessings and your advice to find a right and worthy match for my daughter," responded Kakudmi. He then pulled out a small piece of rolled cloth which had something written on it.

He opened that cloth and said, "O lord, these are the list of bachelors back on earth. Please suggest who amongst them is the suitable match for Revati."

Revati, with her eyes looking down and folded hands, was listening to the conversation, without interfering them.

Hearing this, Brahma broke into a huge laughter.

"Ha ha ha. You innocent beings from earth! By the time you spent here, several chatur-yugas have passed on in earth. All these people whose names you have written in there are long gone. So are their descendants," said Brahma.

"What? what... how can that be...we are here only for about three-quarters of a muhurta..." Kakudmi said, while stammering a little. He was losing his nerves, but maintaining his composure. The balance between fear and courage is a difficult act and Kakudmi was doing his best in this. Revati was equally astonished and dismayed by this revelation.

"Yes, in this three quarters muhurta in Brahma Lok, twenty-seven chatur yugas have passed on earth. Currently, it is twenty-eighth chatur-yuga, and it is the Dwapar-Yuga of this Maha-Yug," said Brahma.

Father and daughter looked at each other, looking for solace in each other's eyes. The truth was slowly sinking in.

"So, what is your blessing for us, O dear lord," asked Revati, who was silent all this while.

"Dear Revati, in the Dwapar of the twenty-eighth Maha-Yug, Shree Vishnu has incarnated as Shree Krishna and his Seshnag as his elder brother, Balram. I bless you to be the wife of Balram."

"Your blessing is our driving force," said Revati with folded hands.

"And one more thing, King and Princess. The two ghosts whom you have brought in here make use of them when you go back to earth. Do not worry about sending them back. You can do that anytime. Your craft has been re-fuelled with sufficient Amrit to take you back and cover for their return," advised Brahma.

"I do not get that, O lord. How to use them?" asked Kakudmi, puzzled by the intriguing suggestion of Brahma.

"That you will figure out when you face the need." Brahma paused a bit and continued. "I would now suggest you both to board the craft and start your return trip before it is too late."

Hearing this, Kakudmi and Revati bid farewell to the Supreme Creator and turned back to move out of the Palace and towards their craft.

CHAPTER 14

THE DWAPAR

Back on the ship, Jay and Professor Doherty's *ghosts* were peeping outside of all the windows, trying to get the best possible views of an alien planet. Never had they imagined that they would be served with such eye-delicacies. The beautiful, yet sophisticated land was surprising them every instant.

Strange looking creatures, swiftly moving vehicles, ordered civilians and the best usage of technology alongside the cozy nature was enough to absorb them.

"We saw the technology in our world and witnessed the natural beauty in Kakudmi's kingdom, but nothing is so awesome as this place," an awestruck Jay spoke to Professor.

"Do not forget we are on an alien planet, Jay."

Professor continued, "see how best scientific development is flourishing without harming the nature. This is something we need to learn and teach our world when we get back."

"Do you think, Professor, people would believe us when we tell this story to them?" Jay asked a very obvious question.

"You have a point, Jay. But we need to tell this learning, whether as a true story or a fiction. We cannot hide this gem from the world. Many people would not believe you, maybe a majority of them, but there would definitely be some who may find interest in your stories and they would do their best to spread what they believe. Even if you can change one person, believe me, that is worth it."

"But how are we going to learn ourselves, sir?"

"Ask questions. Ask from this King. He is a wise man, and a knowledgeable at the same time. Learn from him," said Doherty.

And they heard the sound of steps coming in closer to the ship. In the next moment they could see Revati and Kakudmi hurrying in to the ship and hastening to the bridge level.

By the time they joined the king and the princess on the third level bridge, the ship had already come off the ground and was speeding up at a tremendous speed.

***

"Thank you, dear spirits, for obeying me and keeping your promise," said Kakudmi as he sensed both the souls nearing him.

"We are men of words, O King," said the professor.

Professor Doherty then continued, "may I ask if you found what you came here for and did you get how to refuel this vehicle?"

"Yes, and Yes. But there are *things* that have happened and more are going to happen in the coming days," responded Kakudmi.

On further asking, Kakudmi revealed the time dilation effect they would undergo and as a result would land on earth not in the time they left, but many Yugas later.

"So, we are getting closer to the time where we belong," said Jay sarcastically.

Kakudmi replied, "yes, but that is not going to help you either. You need to get back to your time, not closer to it. Moreover, you need to return to your dimension where you can get your physical self, where you can breathe. There is no point returning to your time yet not being able to touch yourself."

"Very true, dear king," said Jay.

"Dear king, as you know this is going to be a long trip back home, can we utilize this time and gain some wisdom from you," requested Jay.

"Oh, that is so good to be coming from you. I appreciate your zeal," said Kakudmi.

"Let me know what you would like to know."

"We saw the advancement of Brahma-Lok. Can you enlighten us on how we can achieve the advancement of Brahma-Lok?" asked Jay.

Kakudmi organized his thought over this question; he kept silent for a few moments and then said, "getting the best benefits of science and avoiding its curse is an art. It is unfortunate that humans rarely learn this art. And where they understand and practice this, they do it on an individual level and not at the community level."

"And the way to learn this art is by *dharma*, by following the path of virtue and righteousness and not letting the evil thought dwell in you."

"How is the possible, sir? How can we control our fickle mind?" asked Jay.

"By performing *yog*, and by controlling our senses. There is a Vedic verse that says - *aham brahmasmi* - meaning there is an entity of God within me and within every living being. When you start practicing this, you begin to see God in everyone. And when you see that, you would have respect, love, and empathy for everyone. That is the key to learn the art of humanity. And only then you can control your mind," explained the king.

"Thank you for explaining that to me, O King."

Jay further continued with another question. "Dear King, you mentioned that practicing this art has been done at an individual level and not at a community level. If that is the case, how have the residents of Brahma Lok achieved this?"

"That is a very good question, dear friend. Residents of Brahma Lok are no ordinary beings. They are the most knowledgeable and wise people from their world. Wise people from various worlds of this Universe get the opportunity to reside in this great place of knowledge and be a part of its governance. After all, they are running the knowledge hub of the Universe. So, they have the capability and wisdom to garner only the good effects of science."

Jay and Professor Doherty spent their time on their return travel to gain as much knowledge as they could. Sometimes they were awestruck at their learning, at other times they had a realization at how simple and obvious things can be, if looked from the right perspective.

***

After travel of about a month, their craft landed on earth. They landed exactly at the same co-ordinates as they had taken off. The only difference this time was the place was no more a Royal Palace or an underground basement. Rather, it was a barren land next to the sea.

Revati and Kakudmi exited the craft, so did the two ghosts.

"Father, is this the place we lived in our Yug?" asked Revati.

"It seems like, but in our time, the sea was far away from our palace. Look how close the sea has come," said Kakudmi.

Both of them walked away from the sea, trying to find people. Jay and Professor Doherty also levitated following the King.

As they went a few meters away, they could hear horse's steps closing in. They were attentive as they were venturing in a different time altogether. Soon they could see some soldiers riding on their horses coming near.

The horses came close to them and stopped. Alighted four soldiers. The soldiers were much sorter in height than Kakudmi and Revati.

One of them came near to Kakudmi, looked up to the King's chin and said, "Who are you? Prove your identity."

"From a far-off place, we have arrived here. We do not mean to harm you or your people. We just wish to meet your king," replied Kakudmi.

"Okay, but you need to prove your identity. Let us know who are you and what purpose brings you here?"

"My name is Kakudmi, and I was the King of a state named Kushasthali. We ventured out to explore the world and now I do not have my kingdom," said Kakudmi and then he pointed towards his daughter and said, "and she is my daughter, Revati."

Revati, who was silent all this while, stepped two steps forward and asked the soldier, "what kingdom is this and who is your king?"

"O Lady, this is Dwarka. And our king is Shree Krishna."

Soldier further directed them to come with them and said, "you need to come with us as you shall have the trial in the Kingdom's court."

The soldiers also looked towards their ship and said, "we are also taking your ship into our custody, and now both of you follow us."

Two of the soldiers stayed near the ship, guarding it against any infiltration or misuse. The other two climbed their horses and offered the two horses to Kakudmi and Revati. All four of them moved away from the sea and towards the city of Dwarka.

***

As they moved closer to the city, the crowds thickened. The city looked wealthy and harmony flowed in the air.

"The people of this *Yug* are smaller than our times, father," said Revati.

"That is the effect of Yug change, Revati. With every passing yug, beings and their dharma diminish. You would also find many things different here," said Kakudmi.

"Like what, father?"

"Like people would be untrustworthy, there would be more of evil qualities in humans than the goodness. People would be lying and misery would surmount everywhere. So, be very careful, O dear."

Kakudmi moved his horse closer to one of the soldiers and said, "my friend, how far we going to ride before we reach the King's Palace?"

"Sir, you are not going to the Palace. You both are our prisoners. You would be taken to the courtroom," responded the soldier. Kakudmi and Revati did not expect this. They were taken aback. They used to rule this land and now they are taken as prisoners.

"What?" said Revati.

"We are not criminals, neither we did anything wrong. How can we be your prisoners?" Revati said, raising her voice. She was still coming to the terms that she was no more a princess.

"You both are not the citizens of this place and you also have not proven your identity. We need to take you to the courtroom and then you will be served justice accordingly," said the soldier.

Soon they reached the government building, heavily protected by armoured soldiers. They got down from the horses and walked in to that building.

It was quite evident from their looks that Revati and Kakudmi were not really enjoying the things in the Dwapar.

In the meantime, Jay and the Professor were witnessing all the events, and they finally decided to be with Kakudmi so that they could be of any help for him. After all, Kakudmi was the key to their return travel.

CHAPTER 15

SHREE KRISHNA

Revati and Kakudmi walked in, escorted by the two soldiers. They entered the courtroom.

Just in front of the entrance was the King's throne on a raised platform. There were two rows of chairs, looking at each other on the two sides of the hall.

It was a large hall, with people all around. Some were sitting on the chair, others standing behind those chairs.

There were balconies on the two walls. On the balconies were seated queens and princess of the kingdom and their maids taking care of them.

However, everyone in the room looked dwarf as compared to Kakudmi and Revati.

Both of them were asked by the soldiers to stand in one corner. They stood there silently, looking all around. And everyone was gazing at them with a strange look, as if they were seeing an alien being. In fact, they were seeing someone who had travelled to a different world and came back travelling through time.

And there was an announcement.

"King of Dwarka, Lord of this world, Shree Krishna is coming to the courtroom!"

Everyone in the room stood on their feet with respect and adoration. They stood up not because of the fear, rather out of love for their king. Some of them stood on their toes to get the best view of their lord.

Krishna walked in with his brother Balram. While Krishna was an ordinary-looking man in dark complexion and average height, his brother was an eight feet giant looking man. He looked very much of same height as Revati and Kakudmi.

Both of them ascended up the stairs of the platform and sat on the two thrones. One of those thrones, being higher and grander, signifying the King's place. Krishna occupied that seat.

"Please start the proceedings," said Krishna, looking around the courtroom.

"Sir, we have the first case of two unknown people found in our kingdom who arrived in their strange looking craft," said the courtroom spokesman.

The soldiers meanwhile pushed Kakudmi towards the centre of the hall, while Revati stood at the corner.

Looking at Krishna, Kakudmi remembered his conversation with Brahma.

He is Narayan, the param-brahm.

The thought ran through his mind, and he bowed in front of Krishna.

He said in his self - *Om Vishnave Namaha.*

Krishna looked at them, smiled at him and Revati as if he knew everything, yet he said, "Please let us know who are you?"

"*Namaskar*, O dear King. I am Kakudmi, the king of Kushasthali and she is my daughter, Revati."

Balram was not at all entertained by hearing this. He immediately said with little anger, "what do you mean? Kushasthali is the old name of Dwarka and you are saying you are king of Dwarka."

Balram was a short-tempered person, and he was also quick to react. Krishna, on the other hand, was much more stable and maintained the pose. He looked towards his brother in his eyes and closed his own eyes, signalling to keep calm.

Balram understood the subtle language.

Krishna then said, "and what is your purpose to come here, dear King Kakudmi?"

"I am here with my daughter, Revati," said Kakudmi and gestured his hand towards Revati, who was standing a few feet away. Revati walked up to his father and greeted Krishna, "Namaskar".

Kakudmi continued, "I am here to get the right match for my daughter and to get her married before taking to penance for myself. My fatherly duty has compelled to travel through time and reach the present day Kushasthali called Dwarka."

Balram was meanwhile awestruck by the beauty and personality of the Princess. He could not take his eyes off Revati. He had never seen so tall, well-built and beautiful lady. Her voice was echoing in his ears.

"Very well, dear Kakudmi and Revati. You are my guest. We should have welcomed you instead of bringing you to this courtroom. We are sorry for this treatment," said Krishna.

Krishna further continued directing the officers of the court and to the soldiers, "I order to take off all charges from them, and respectfully they should be hosted at our Royal Palace. They are our guests."

"Please accept our hospitality. You have had a long journey. We will talk further once settle in."

***

In the meantime, Jay and Professor Doherty returned to the Vimana for their stay while in Dwarka. They did not want to be away from their ride.

Upon arrival at the Royal palace, Kakudmi and Revati received all the comforts that a royal guest was given.

In the palace they were welcomed by Vaidehi, who was an employee of the palace and took care of the guests.

That full day they spent sleeping and coming off the time-dilation effect their bodies had. They relaxed in the specially designed jacuzzi pool, ate and drank best Ayurvedic preparations to help them with nutrition and relaxation.

The materialistic lifestyle was much enjoyable when they compared with the times of Satya-Yug.

"Those were the primitive time, dear father," said Revati when they were sitting for the evening dinner.

"Everything has evolved with time, and humans have created many instruments of pleasure. This would only increase in the coming time," replied Kakudmi.

He further continued, "by the way, how do you find Balram?"

Revati did not have a good first-time interaction with Balram. She only got the feel of his short-tempered nature. But whatever she observed, she was more inclined towards making an opinion. She could not convince herself that their travel would be fruitful at all.

"I can't say, father. I have been thinking that whole day, but I cannot convince myself."

She continued, "but even then, I would say let us give some time to this. Lord Brahma cannot be a wrong guide. He is the creator god and preserver of Vedas."

"Wise words, daughter."

While they were having dinner, Vaidehi walked in.

She said, "our king wants to meet you. He would like to know when can he come over?"

Revati and Kakudmi were surprised as the King of the state was asking for their permission.

"We can do it now, if it is good with Krishna," said Revati.

"Sure, I shall inform the king that you are available for the meeting now," said Vaidehi before making her way out.

"He did not call us, rather he is visiting us in here. Such is the greatness and humbleness of the king. He can be no other than Shree Vishnu," said Kakudmi.

***

"Namaskar, O' Vasudev," greeted Kakudmi as Krishna entered the guest room of the Palace.

Krishna responded with a big smile and warm aura that he was carrying with him, "Namaskar, King of Kushasthali."

Kakudmi and Revati stood up regarding the all-powerful and supreme being. There was something in the presence of Krishna that was making everyone at peace in the room.

"How are you both doing now? Hope you had a good repose after a tiring journey," said Krishna.

"We were anxious before seeing you, but your presence is so much soothing and relaxing, Krishna, that I am now assured we have come to the right place," said Kakudmi.

"What brings you here? Help me understand your purpose."

This time it was Revati who responded, "we lived in Kushasthali twenty-seven *mahayugs* ago. For meeting Brahma-dev, we departed this planet and on coming back, we found that Kushasthali had changed to Dwarka."

Revati paused for a moment, looking at the smiling Krishna and said further, "we were advised by the supreme creator of this Universe that I would be finding my husband as your brother Balram. But I am not very sure if indeed Brahma-dev was right."

"Brahma-dev cannot be wrong. By the way, that is an interesting story and be assured we would do whatever it takes to fulfil Brahms-dev's suggestion," responded Krishna. And as he spoke this, his emotions changed gradually to a more serious tone and composure.

Krishna further continued, "we would be happy to consider this alliance, just that few things need to be taken care of before we get into this auspicious solemnity."

"And what are those things, Krishna?" asked Kakudmi.

"We are seeing multiple threats right now from many enemy states. Both of us, me and my brother, are in Dwarka now and it has come to my information that Jarasandh and Kalyavan are planning an attack on Mathura."

Jarasandh was father-in-law of Kansh, Krishna's maternal uncle whom Krishna killed and ended his evil kingship. Thus, he had freed people of Mathura from the cruel hands of Kansh. After Kansh's death, Jarasandh was eyeing the control of this neighbour state and hence was planning its accession. He had tried several times but every time his attempt was foiled by the strong *Narayani Sena* and tactful strategies of Krishna.

After several such failed attempts, Jarasandh decided to take help from his friend from Yavan, the king of Yavan called Kalyavan.

"So, who is Kalyavan and why is he posing such a big danger to Mathura?" asked Revati.

"Kalyavan is not an ordinary king. He is a great devotee of Brahma and Mahadev. He took a severe penance in devotion to Mahadev and thus was blessed that he would be invincible in the war; no one can defeat him, not even me," answered Krishna with deep and thoughtful voice.

"As an immediate measure to tackle the attack, I shall be departing tomorrow for Mathura. Let us solve the incoming danger first. Until then, we will have to wait and postpone all our ceremonies."

As the picture was becoming clear, Revati began to connect the dots and understand the purpose. She offered her assistance in the war, saying,

"Let us know if you need any help."

"Thank you for those good words. I shall let you know if we need any help," said Krishna before exchanging greetings and departing from there.

CHAPTER 16

BALRAM

The next morning Revati was taking a leisure walk in the Palace Garden. Vaidehi was giving her the company. She was also acting as her guide.

Coming from a different era, Revati had many questions trying to understand the culture, purpose and reason behind everything. She was a curious mind and how can she keep her questions suppressed.

"Vaidehi, what does your name mean? I have never heard of this name before," said Revati while touching the flowers in the garden.

Vaidehi felt surprised at her ignorance. But she did not show any of that surprise and said, "Vaidehi is another name for Sita, the wife of Shree Ram."

"Would you like to tell me more about Vaidehi?" asked Revati. Revati had not heard of Ramayan because she had skipped the Treta Yug altogether. She left earth in Satya Yug and returned while it was Dwapar Yug. And because of this, she was not aware of Ramayan, Ram, or Sita.

"In the Treta-Yug, the princess of Videh state was Sita. She was from the Videh and hence was also called as Vaidehi. She was married to Shree Ram of Ayodhya. It is said that Ram was an incarnation of Shree Vishnu and Mata Sita was the incarnation of the goddess Laxmi," responded Vaidehi.

She further added as a suggestion, "you should read the epic of Ramayan sometime. It is a treasure of knowledge."

"Sure, I would," said Revati, as she moved towards the *Peepal* tree in the centre of the garden. She stood there under the shadow of the tree when her eyes fell on the group of citizens standing in the courtyard next to the garden. Talking with them was the tall and handsome Balram.

"Who are these people, Vaidehi?" asked Revati.

"They are the farmers, dear lady. They would have come for asking some help with the prince. Our prince Balram is a very benevolent and humble natured. He is always there to help the poor and oppressed of the society. He carries a plough as his weapon, something that connects him to the common farmer, rather than carrying a *Kshatriya* weapon. By the way, there was news of flood in the regions along Saraswati River, the mightiest river of this land. So, these people are probably from there."

Vaidehi further added, "he is one of the most powerful and strong warriors this earth has. No one has ever defeated him in wrestling and in the fight of mace."

Those words from Vaidehi were starting to change Revati's heart. She was beginning to like Balram. But it was just the beginning. She had a long way to go before drawing the complete character of Balram on the canvas within her heart.

***

Balram, on the other side of the garden, was discussing a grave matter with the farmers. He has been protecting the farms and animals of his province from the demons and asuras who used to loot the poor villagers. But now he was poised with the challenge of the flood.

"Do not worry, dear friends. Let me see how to solve the flood issue." Balram assured his people, "as of now, I am directing all possible help from our treasury to the people of affected areas."

"*Jai ho Haldhar*," said the villagers before dissipating and walking out.

As the people left, Revati and Vaidehi walked towards Balram.

Revati had gathered all the information, in the meantime, from Vaidehi and her other friends at work.

Revati's sight had a serene impact on the face of Balram. His stress faded away by the mere look of the beautiful eyes. Revati's beauty captivated him. Revati's voice, however, brought him back to senses.

"Is there anything troubling you?" asked Revati, and further added, "if I may be of any help to your purpose then I may consider myself blessed."

"No, it is nothing that serious. We will take care of it."

"You may confide in me. And let me tell you I am a trained warrior. I have the blessing of meeting Vaivasvat Manu, and have received warfare training from him. I can be relied upon, if you wish to use my services," said Revati.

Revati was a helping and empathetic person. When she found herself capable of doing her bit, she never retreated her step. And she loved challenges. She could have not missed helping Balram in this instance.

"That is so kind of you to come forward for help, even when you are a guest in this kingdom. However, I can take care of this," said Balram.

"O, you surely do. I do not doubt that. But I leave the decision up to you. I do not want to put you in any awkward situation. But I shall be available to serve this kingdom in time when it is needed," replied Revati firmly. Revathi exchanged greetings before leaving the garden.

Balram liked her confidence. He could not stop himself from thinking of her, even after she was gone from the scene.

Balram was enchanted by a unique chemical running within his head. He was lost in love. He was feeling the lovely fragrance of the beautiful flowers that were blossoming within himself.

***

While Balram was taking care of the people affected by the nature's fury, Krishna was preparing to depart on his grand chariot to Mathura. He rode the chariot pulled by a sturdy pair of white horses and his friend Satyaki was his charioteer.

He was followed by one battalion of Narayani Sena, which comprised several horse-riders, elephants and thousands of soldiers who were marching along.

The month-long journey had many stoppages, crossing over several cities along the banks of rivers and lakeshores on the way.

In those days, battalions were prepared to travel for months with many stoppages. Where ever they stopped, there was a kind of festive celebration of some short with food being cooked, alcohols brewed and dance and music performed. The troops carried all the required livestock along with them and that is how a big-sized battalion was fed and kept energetic.

CHAPTER 17

SARASWATI

"The loss has been huge, my lady. Thousands of village people have lost their lives," said Vaidehi as she explained the devastating flood on the river Saraswati.

"Natural calamities have always been devastating. Don't know when we can win over these things," Revati was sad and with the feeling that she could not help, was more regretful. However, the feeling of empathy was overwhelming her, and she was growing restless. She wanted to visit the flood affected areas to assess the situation herself, but she was not aware of the geography and the coordinates of the region. It had changed significantly since the time of Kushasthali.

Revati went to Kakudmi to discuss if they could do a survey and help the villagers. Kakudmi was talking to Jay and Professor's ghosts who were also getting restless as they were worried about the time-dilation effect between the dimension. They had their own miseries.

"Father, did you hear about the flood?" asked Revati.

Kakudmi had his eyes closed while he was communicating with the matrix walkers. He said to them - *Do not be restless, dear souls. We have come along so far and I am seeing your transition not very far away. You shall receive what you want once my mission gets over.*

Kakudmi opened his eyes and looked towards Revati. Grief and trouble were visible on her face.

"I have heard of floods, dear Revati, but mother nature is unleashing her wrath and we are powerless in the face of this act of god," Kakudmi responded.

"I know that, father," said Revati, "but what I want is to assess the impact and then create a strategy for helping those whose lives are affected."

"Very well, let us discuss with Balram."

***

Balram was all ears for Revati's desire. He formed a group of swimmers and boatmen to navigate through the flooded regions.

Balram, along with Revati and Kakudmi, toured over the angry waters in a boat that he brought.

Jay also hovered above the boat. While Professor chose to stay on the Shree Vimana, Jay was looking to stray out to douse his anxiety.

They reached the village where flood water had reached and where the boat was waiting for them.

On the way, they could see people crying out loud, mourning the death of their dear ones. An old woman was sitting beside the dead bodies of her son- and daughter-in-law. A man carrying his motionless child in his hands, shouting for the child to wake up. People looking out for their missing family members in the camps set up by the kingdom's government. There was chaos, mourning, sadness everywhere. Death was dancing all around.

Revati was crying out loud. She had never seen destruction of such magnitude in her life. Kakudmi was dumb silent. Balram was calm and directed his soldiers and officers to help the villagers wherever possible.

Going further into the water, they navigated through the boat. On the way, they could see hundreds of dead bodies floating in the water. Men, women and children were amongst the dead.

Jay was also in a shock. Seeing the death all around, he forgot their own misery. However, he had more eerie experiences. He was not only seeing dead bodies all around, but was also seeing spirits levitating around. He could hear them cry, shout, and talk.

One of those spirits came closer and said, *"you seem to be a royal spirit, please help us."*

Jay looked towards the manly figure, and said, *"but you seem to be dead already. What help you need?"*

"The ghosts of unnatural death are us. We are stuck between the two dimensions. We are neither from this earthly dimension nor from the pitri-lok. We are stuck. Help us..."

Jay felt shocked. This was the first time he was having a *spiritual* experience with ghosts. With many questions engulfing within, Jay said, *"But why are you stuck? Why do not you follow the same path as others who die?"*

"Don't you know this? Those who die an unnatural death like sudden accident, natural calamity and by suicide are stuck. Performing the last rites will lead to our release. However, those who die by suicide do not have an escape. They are stuck in here for many thousands of years."

Hearing this, Jay went in a deep thought. He himself was attempting a suicide some days back. Had he known this truth, he would have never allowed that thought to live in his head. *Thank God that you sent Patricia that day*, he thought.

Jay held his thoughts for a moment. He took a deep pause and said, *"do not worry my friend. I will make sure to pass on your message to the right people, so that they can perform the last rites with utmost care and at the earliest."*

In the meantime, Balram and his officials noted the living people who needed help. Subsequently, help was sent to them. The soldiers and officials also collected all the dead bodies that were floating.

Jay looked towards Kakudmi and said, "King Kakudmi, are you seeing these spirits like I am seeing?"

Kakudmi looked to his right and responded, "I can sense them, but I cannot see."

"They are stuck in here. They are demanding their last rites to be performed," said Jay.

"Thanks for letting me know. We shall get this done soon," responded Kakudmi. He then passed on the message to Balram and Revati. Balram made sure all the dead bodies were respectfully retrieved and burned with all *dharmic* rituals.

Supplies of food, medicine and other necessities were also sent to the survivors. Several camps were built in the kingdom to take care of the dislocated villagers.

In a few more days, the water subsided. River gave back the land it had acquired from the villagers. Peace and resources came back, but the scar that was left in the hearts was hard to remove. Most people were more accepting than questioning. However same was not true for everyone. Revati was brainstorming to find a permanent solution.

***

"I am indebted to you for your advice, my dear Revati," said Balram.

All three of them were in the palace, while Jay went to the Professor to share his experiences.

"You do not need to thank me. Anyone at my place would

have done the same. We are just the mere tools; *he* is the one who is sending us where we go," said Revati, thanking the God who keeps everyone in his shelter.

"That is your greatness, and that makes me love and respect more about you," Balram was admiring the company of Revati.

"But we need to find some solution to the flood havocs. There has to be some solution to prevent such devastation in the future," Revati said, looking towards Balram and Kakudmi.

Suddenly something clicked in her mind and she said, "why do not we ask from the matrix-walkers, as they are from the dimension from the future? I am sure the future would not be the same. Coming generations, they would device something that would prevent such havoc."

"Hmm... yes, you are right."

"We have the company of the two matrix-walkers from the future. Why not make use of them to know what preventions and safety measure they take?"

"Oh yes, that is a brilliant point," said Kakudmi and apprised Balram about the event of Jay and Professor Doherty.

"I would say let us not waste anytime seeking the advice, dear king Kakudmi and Revati," said Balram.

Balram, Kakudmi and Revati soon headed towards the Shree Vimana that was parked beside the sea.

***

The spacecraft was in the same place where it had landed. It was heavily guarded by the soldiers. No one could enter that Vimana. Only Jay and Professor had the twenty-four-hour pass; they were invisible to be detected.

Balram, Revati and Kakudmi entered the Vimana. Balram was astonished by the technology of the Vimana.

"So, this is the craft that was used by Manu to save humanity when there was *Pralay*," said Balram.

"Oh yes, it is," replied Revati with a little pride and a lot of gratitude.

"Please be seated, by the time I communicate with *them*," said Kakudmi.

All three of them occupied the chairs kept around the panel, having glowing lights and buttons.

"I hope you are doing well, Jay and Doherty," asked Kakudmi, closing his eyes.

"Jay is in shock. He is taking time to come back to senses after what he saw near the river," said Professor Doherty.

"I can understand. He saw even that which we could not. Let him be at peace. But I need some answers from you," said Kakudmi.

"Let me know what you want to know?" asked Professor Doherty.

"How in your times do you avoid flood?"

"Even in our world, we do not have a full-proof solution, however we have made dams that could control the river might."

Kakudmi listened to each word very carefully and further asked, *"please can you elaborate that?"*

"Sure, I will. These are mega-structures built around a part of the river, usually around a river valley, that can hold immense quantities of water. That way, we control the excess water that flows in and allow only a limited amount to flow out."

"Do you have any design for that?"

"Allow me to connect to the internet of our age from Shree Vimana and we can get the complete design and architecture."

"Okay, please go ahead."

Kakudmi then spoke to Shree Vimana and asked to help Professor Doherty.

Professor gave the web address of one of the papers he had co-authored with his friend and an architect. This was the paper that had details on how dams are being constructed and how modern days dams are similar in design to the ancient dams found in India.

In a moment, Shree Vimana pulled out that article written by Professor Doherty. The information was displayed on the screen of the Vimana, along with the QR code of the webpage. As the information was in English, Professor Doherty communicated with Kakudmi to pass on the message. Kakudmi noted that in a piece of *Tal Patra*.

Kakudmi wrote every bit of detail and drew the diagrammatic structure.

He further also drew the QR code that was displayed.

"You can ignore the square picture. That is a QR code. It is used to retrieve the information. You may not need that," said Professor Doherty.

"Oh, that is fine. We may use this as an insignia. Thank you for your help," said Kakudmi.

With all the required information, Kakudmi, Balram, and Revati departed from the spacecraft.

Professor Doherty was having the feeling of goosebumps as he was able to connect some more dots, and thus was able to solve one more riddle - the QR code scripted on the archaeological epithets.

CHAPTER 18

MUCHAKUND

With the design in hand, Balram brought in the best of the workers and engineers he had in the whole of Bharat. The site for the construction of the dam was strategically chosen near the city of Dhaula. Saraswati river on its way to the sea, crossed the Kutcha region of Dhaula and during flood this was the region that saw maximum devastation.

Shri Krishna was informed, who was preparing for a long battle in Mathura. He was happy that Balram and Revati were working together to build a mega-structure of the future. He provided all the required support and permission to get the things started.

But while things were sorted out in Dwarka, there were challenges building up over Mathura.

City of Mathura was very different from Dwarka. The main reason being this city was much older. The layers of the city were built one over the other. Whereas with most other cities, including Dwarka, those were built, broken down, re-built again. So, the façade of the buildings looked very new and shiny in the case of Dwarka, but Mathura looked much older with red clay bricks lining on the roads and the buildings. The doors were not very sophisticated and streets were as clumsy as they could be. The city was protected as a fortress, with tall walls on all sides.

Mathura was also very densely populated, so the chaos on the streets was very high. People moving around at their own pace and motives. Everyone looked busy. And this was an important indicator of the economic development. The city was a business hub of the time. Travellers and traders came attracted from various parts of the world.

When the Narayani Sena entered the city of Mathura, they were welcomed by the soldiers and employees of the government.

As they reached outside the King's Mahal, Krishna jumped off his chariot. He was welcomed by Uddhav, a dear friend of Krishna and a commander of the army.

"Namaste, Madhav," said Uddhav. Uddhav was a friend to Krishna and was of the same age. He called Krishna by another name of Madhav.

"Namaste, dear Uddhav. How are our deployments now?"

"We are guarded by *Chaturanga* formation of our armies. Deployment is on all sides. Our one hundred Narayani Sena units have been deployed outside the gates on all sides, whereas another one hundred are kept at the gates. We also have an equal number in reserve," responded Uddhav.

"Very good. I would like to see all these deployments myself. Can you arrange for a visit later this afternoon, please?"

"Sure, Madhav."

"And one more thing. I feel we should strengthen our position in the east. Jarasandh would attack us, probably from the east. So, let us surprise him by digging a trench in our east, much outside of our city, around fifty miles away. And position a few units of our soldiers near that trench," said Balram.

"As you say, my friend."

Krishna and Uddhav talked more about the strategies and the oncoming enemy. They moved inside the Mahal.

***

Back in Dwarka, Revati and Kakudmi were now aware of the warlike situation that was building up in Mathura. They were worried about the upcoming war and the kingdom's safety in Dwarka. Both of them were a great warrior of their time and they wanted to lend their support to Krishna and Balram.

They walked in to Balram's chamber and were greeted by Balram as if he was expecting them.

"Namaste Balram," greeted Kakudmi.

"Namaste, O' King of Kushasthali, and dear Princess. Hope you are doing well. Please do not hesitate if you need anything," responded Balram.

"We are very good, thanks to your hospitality. Just this thought of not being of any help in this upcoming time of crisis is not letting us breath in peace," said Revati.

Balram gestured both of them to be seated on the chairs beside his own royal seat.

"Your travel through yugas was destined. Your presence in this time, place, and situation was also pre-determined. Nothing in this world happens for no reason. We have to witness how the things unfold and you will be able to help the time," said Balram.

Balram looked at Kakudmi and continued, "by the way do you have any message from Shree Brahma for me or Krishna? My brother thinks that you may have some valuable message from Lord Brahma for us."

Kakudmi remembered the meeting and talk they had with Brahma, in which he had said to reveal a location to Krishna, but only when he was asked about it. This was the reason Kakudmi and Revati were seeking such an opportunity to render their help. They had asked several times if their help and contribution were needed.

Kakudmi hesitated and said, "Oh, yes, dear Balram. He has given a location to be revealed on being asked."

"Okay, and what that is?" asked Balram.

"That is *Muchakund Gufa*, a cave where King Muchakund of Ikshvaku dynasty is in sleep. The one who wakes him up will be burnt to ashes when Muchakund lays his eyes on that person. That is all we know," said Kakudmi.

Balram was happy to receive the information from Brahma-Lok, but he was not very sure how to use that. He instantly called a messenger so that the information could be sent to Mathura.

"Thank you so much, king Kakudmi. I hope this information may be of some use to Krishna," said Balram.

Balram pulled out a Tal Patra from the stack kept on the table. He wrote some lines before sticking it on the silk envelope and then rolling it. He handed over that letter to the messenger and asked him to carry the message to Mathura and deliver to none other than Krishna.

***

Everyday sunrise brought a new challenge for Mathura. Jarasandh wanted to weaken the Mathura army to the point that when Kalyavan attacks, he would be victorious. Jarasandh was sending the best of his commanders and was launching the deadly weapons on Krishna and his army.

Jarasandh had a long-time enmity with Krishna and Balram, ever since Krishna killed Kansh. Kansh was married to two daughters of Jarasandh, Asti and Prapti.

Jarasandh wanted to revenge Kansh's death, and hence he attacked Mathura multiple times. On being unsuccessful in many attempts, he finally built an alliance with the King of Yavan, Kalyavan. Kalyavan was supposed to be very powerful demon. His might and power were known world-wide and when Jarasandh got an opportunity to befriend him, he did not let go that chance. He initially had a trade relation with Yavan and later became a good friend of his. On the other hand, Kalyavan wanted to gain control of *Bharat-bhumi,* the land mass of the Indian subcontinent. And he knew that with Krishna present in Bharat, he would never be able to succeed in this endeavour.

Enemy of an enemy often becomes friends. And the same happened yet again.

***

Meanwhile, the messenger from Dwarka reached Mathura in about a week's time. Given the importance of the matter, the speed of travel had to increase many folds.

The messenger handed over the letter to Krishna as soon he arrived in Mathura. As Krishna read the letter, he had a smile on his face. A sense of calmness appeared as he rolled the letter back and kept on the table.

Uddhav was with Krishna. He was curious to know the content of the letter.

"What is it, Madhav?"

"Uddhav, my friend, Revati and Kakudmi have brought a very useful information from Brahma-Lok. I have a way out to defeat Kalyavan."

"Uddhav, any news about the friends and alliances of Jarasandh?" asked Krishna.

"Keshav, as you know, Kalyavan is already on our land. He has also further advanced and come very close to the Khandavprasth. Our spies are constantly following his movements. We expect him to further progress towards our premises in the next couple of weeks. Barring Kalyavan, Jarasandh is all alone," answered Uddhav.

Krishna was often called by his other names. Keshav was one of them.

Khandavprasth was the region ruled by the Pandavas, under the leadership of the eldest of all Pandavas, Yudhisthir.

Krishna was well aware that his chief opponent was not Jarasandh. Krishna was also not worried by the several attacks launched by him. He was wary about the advances Kalyavan was making.

Krishna further said, looking towards Uddhav, "dear brother, we shall continue defending ourselves from Jarasandh the way we are doing. And when Kalyavan comes to our door, I shall welcome him."

Uddhav understood Krishna's instruction. He nodded in agreement.

***

In the next couple of weeks, Uddhav and Krishna rocked the enemies. Jarasandh was no match for their skills. But they knew Jarasandh was only a mock-up. The real enemy was approaching the gates from the other side.

And finally, the day came when Kalyavan with his *black* army reached right outside the premises of Mathura. The colour of the army uniform was black and hence they were referred to as the black army.

***

The two armies were facing one another. One was coloured black whereas other was in red. Warriors were on elephants, chariots, horses, bulls, and on foot. The formations of armies determined their strategies. While Kalyavan was having a triangular formation pointed towards the opponent, the Narayani Sena was having a *Vyuh*, a spiral formation to trap the king within.

The conch was sounded from one side while drums were beaten on the other. Each side had their own rituals and rules to initiate the fight and build motivation in their armies. The flags were rising high and patriotic slogans were shouted on each side.

And then started the fight. Infantry troopers against infantry, elephants against elephants, horses against horses, and chariots against chariots. The arrows and spears filled up the sky intermittently, resulting in the killing of scores of soldiers.

Krishna moved forward with his chariot and closed upon Kalyavan. He shouted Kalyavan for a direct one on one. Kalyavan was also a gallant commander and ruler. He pulled his arrows, fitted between his fingers and set on his bow, launching three arrows at a time. Krishna was using advanced weapons that disintegrated mid-air into multiple arrows and thus neutralized Kalyavan's launches. The fight went on for several hours. No one was lesser. Both were fighting a worthy opponent.

It was then Krishna retreated. He asked his charioteer to pull back and run away from the battleground.

Kalyavan was not happy with this. He wanted to fight and win over the battle. But Krishna had a different plan.

And Kalyavan shouted, "Oh Krishna, you are running away... you coward, come back and fight with me!"

Krishna heard his loud voice and looking back smiled at him. The charioteer of Krishna, Satyaki, followed the instructions of his master. He commanded the horses to run at higher speed.

Seeing Krishna fleeing away, Kalyavan shouted again, "you *Runnchhod*, you are a coward. But I will kill you today. You cannot run away from your death. I am coming..."

Runnchhod literally means one who runs away from the battleground. And after this incident Krishna gained one more name to his collection of names.

Kalyavan then followed Krishna. His charioteer also sped up the horses at great speed. The chase went on for several miles. Kalyavan was also shooting arrows and other *astras* while following his enemy. However, Satyaki was a skilled charioteer and his zig-zag motion escaped being targeted to Kalyavan's weapons.

Soon, Krishna came to a place that was at the base of a mountain and had dense forest surrounding the mountain. He got down his chariot and asked Satyaki to move aside. Kalyavan saw this, and he too moved on his feet, following Krishna.

Krishna climbed up the mountain and came outside a huge cave. He turned back, looking at Kalyavan in his eyes. Kalyavan was red in anger. He wanted to kill Krishna by hook or by crook. Krishna smiled at him and went into the dark cave.

Kalyavan also followed and entered into that darkness. He could hardly see anything inside. He moved further carefully using his hands to feel the walls around and with the help of some light that came in through the mouth of the cave. Going further, he felt someone hiding at one corner. With the faint light, he saw a man lying down and covered with a piece of cloth. He touched that figure and pulled the piece of cloth that was covering that manly figure.

"Oh, so here you are. You cannot escape your death, Krishna. Get up and be ready to die," he shouted out in rage, as he pushed that sleeping man.

And then stood a manly figure, a huge ten feet giant-like man. The aura of that man was so strong that there was a glow around his head. Kalyavan was awestruck, looking at someone who was not Krishna. As that man opened his eyes, he looked at Kalyavan with a fierce sight and Kalyavan was burned to ashes in the next few seconds. He was none other than the King Muchakund.

King Muchakund of the Ikshvaku dynasty was in sleep for ages. And he had a blessing from Indra that one who wakes him up will be burnt to ashes when Muchakund lays his eyes on that person. It was because of this blessing Kalyavan couldn't withstand his sight.

Krishna, who was hiding behind Muchakund, emerged out and came in front of Muchakund. By this time, Muchakund gained his consciousness. He saw Shri Krishna in front of him and he knew it was Shree Vishnu, in the avatar of Krishna. He bowed in front of Krishna.

Krishna blessed him and advised him to perform austerity in the Himalayas, as that was the only way to cleanse the sins and attain *moksha*. Muchakund then went to *Gandhmadan Parvat* and, later, to Badrinath to perform penance.

CHAPTER 19

THE WEDLOCK

Krishna emerged from the cave as the winner. He had executed his war strategy efficiently. The war ended and Jarasandh retreated back to his kingdom. With the death of Kalyavan, his army too went back to their homeland.

The news of Mathura's victory spread all across the country, including Dwarka. Balram, Revati and Kakudmi were delighted to hear the news. The city was lighted with lamps, and sweets were distributed among the citizens. Everyone in Dwarka was in celebrations. After all, their king was victorious, and he was coming back to Dwarka.

The celebration went on for weeks. Everyone was even more jubilant to see Krishna as he arrived in Dwarka. His welcome was a grand one.

As he reached the Palace, Krishna went to Kakudmi and Revati to thank them for helping to win over Kalyavan.

"Without your timely help, it would have been very difficult for me to defeat the powerful demon," said Krishna.

"It was our duty, Krishna. We were just the messengers who carried information from Brahma Lok," responded Kakudmi.

Kakudmi then further said, "I have one request to you, O' Krishna. As the war is over, can we plan the marriage ceremony?"

Krishna smiled. He looked at Kakudmi and Revati. He held Kakudmi's hand and said, "we shall get this done at the earliest. I can very well understand your sense of urgency."

***

In the next couple of days, the wedding was held where Revati and Balram accepted each other in their lives.

The celebration that started with the news of Kalyavan's death continued further till the wedding of Balram and Revati.

Jay and Professor Doherty were also witnessing the wedding ceremonies and the jubilant people dancing and feasting around. The celebrations of the wedding were not only limited to the Palace and the city of Dwarka, but to the entire kingdom.

"Look how people forget their miseries and life moves on," said Jay as they moved across the kingdom of Dwarka.

He was communicating with Professor Doherty. He further added, "only few weeks back there was the dance of death in this kingdom. But now, with the good news, everyone has joined together to be part of a brighter future."

"That is true, Jay. World doesn't stop, neither does it wait for you. It moves on. And it is the duty of people to move with the world," replied the professor.

"That reminds me of our absence from our world. We would be missed back home," Jay said, and he was becoming increasingly despondent with each passing day.

"That is a big question we can only answer after breaking through this dimension. But time is approaching, you see, this marriage is getting solemnized, and that opens the door for our travel," Professor Doherty said as he shared optimism with Jay.

"Anyway, look over there. Seems like rituals are done, but why is Revati crying?"

***

Kakudmi was looking to be at peace. After all, his *karma* was meeting his *Dharma*. He had performed his duties very well. He was happy that he could find a right match for his daughter, although the search transcended across ages and realms. He embraced Revati, who was in tears because she knew the time for her father's departure was approaching fast. Kakudmi consoled his daughter and blessed her with a purposeful life ahead.

He turned towards Balram, held his hand, and expressed his compassion and love.

"Take good care of my daughter, and please forgive her if she does anything wrong," said Kakudmi.

Balram nodded his head in *yes* and clasped Kakudmi's hand to convey how much he cared for Revati.

Shri Krishna was smiling all this while. Kakudmi looked at Krishna and came closer to him.

He folded his hands and said to Krishna, "O' preserver of worlds, I have performed my fatherly duties. I seek your guidance now, as I want to take the path of penance."

Krishna saw a sense of calmness, abandonment and dedication to him, and said, "You have done your karma this far very well, O' king of Kushasthali. Follow the path to *Nar and Narayan*. Head towards Badrinath in the lap of Himalayas. That would be your final destination in this world, and that would open up your gates to *moksha*."

Krishna further continued, "however there are a couple of things you still need to complete before you depart. The matrix walkers and the Shree Vimana."

     Time Travellers of Dwarka

"Yes, dear lord. I have that in my mind. That is the next thing I have to perform. Can you please suggest to me the right place to conceal this Vimana?" said Kakudmi.

"Outside of the city in the south and near the sea, there is a mountain. There is a big cavity on this mountain. Often you would find pride of lions occupying that cave. You can hide your ship in that cave," said Krishna.

***

Everyone bade farewell to King Kakudmi as he walked away. He had got the answer to his question. He reached the Shree Vimana and boarded the ship. Jay and Professor Doherty followed him.

They were hopeful that they could now breakthrough the dimensional barrier.

Kakudmi ordered the Shree Vimana to manoeuvre towards the mountain cave as suggested by Krishna. In no time, they reached the destination. The cave was occupied by the pride but the loud noise and vibration of the Vimana moved the beasts out. The energy radiating out of the ship kept all the creatures out of its premises.

Kakudmi then said to Shree, "Shree, please create the portal and allow these souls to pass through to their realm."

"As you say, dear King," responded Shree. The Vimana started revving with a loud noise. Whirling wind was created above the ship's dashboard. That whirlwind started to become bigger. King Kakudmi was thrown away by the immense force of the wind. Jay and the Professor, on the other hand, were sucked in. The souls that were venturing the multi-dimensions and the memory lanes of the Vimana were now getting churned in the wheel of time and space.

For the next few minutes, the Vimana continued making a loud sound, and then suddenly everything was silent. Kakudmi stood on his feet and looked around. He closed his eyes, trying to sense the ghosts, but he could find none. Kakudmi was relieved. He took a breath of peace and serenity. Having performed all his duties, he was now free to follow his path of *moksha*.

CHAPTER 20

BACK TO THE REALM

Jay gained his consciousness. He was lying on the floor of the Shree Vimana. He moved his head to either side. His head was aching profusely, and he was feeling too weary. He pulled himself and stood on his feet, taking the support of the walls of Shree Vimana. He could see water outside of the gates of the Vimana. Blue and green lights blinked on the dashboard of the Vimana. He looked around for Professor Doherty.

Jay could see the Professor was lying a few feet away on the ship's floor. He walked to the Professor and shook his hand and body.

"Professor, wake up…"

"He has not arrived yet. It is only you who has made to this side, O' dear Manu," echoed the voice of Shree.

"What? What does that mean? And why are you calling me Manu?"

"You made it this way because you had to. You are the next Manu of this universe. In the coming days, the world will know you as *Savarni Manu*, Mr Swarney," Shree answered and continued, "Professor Doherty could not make it. He would have landed on some other dimension. I am sorry, Manu, but this was not in my capacity. I can only open portals. The path is decided by destiny. And destiny by one's *karma*."

Jay was not able to speak properly. He was sad, frightened and anxious. He stammered and said, "what… what am I… supposed to do… now?"

"You shall have my services all throughout your life. But you cannot use me for your own materialistic desires. You can only use me when your humankind needs me, just like Vaivasvat and Kakudmi did. Also, you can lead a normal life the way you were doing. And when humanity needs me, you know where to find me," said Shree.

Jay pulled Professor's body, trying to take it out of the Vimana. Just then a huge blow of air wave pushed Jay and Professor's dead body out of the Vimana. Vimana then went invisible. Jay had put on his diver's mask and he swam out of the cave to the sea surface.

Getting on the surface, he raised his hand, signalling the crew on the deck.

"Hey, it's Jay. Let's pull him out," shouted Patricia.

Jay was pulled out of the water. He was relieved to see his friends. He took off his mask and headgear and looked at Patricia with teary eyes.

"What's the matter, Jay? And where were you? You were also out of the network." asked Patricia. Steve and Seth were looking astonishingly at Jay and Patricia.

"Professor," said Jay.

"What happened to him? Where is he?" asked Patricia further.

"He is no more. He is under the sea in the cave," said Jay in a low voice.

Hearing this, Seth instructed the local divers to jump and bring back the Professor's body. Patricia held Jay's hand and pulled him inside the ship. Jay was still in shock and was trying the assimilate all that happened to him all this while. Suddenly, he remembered to ask the most important question that he had been thinking over some time back.

"How much time was I under the sea?"

"You were there slightly more than 3 hours. It is now going to be evening, and we were worried because you were not reachable," answered Patricia.

With a cup of coffee, Jay was getting back to normal. He had experienced several life-times in the brief span of 3 hours, and he had lost his dear professor and friend. He was still coming to terms with it.

***

And they returned. With the unfinished assignment and loads of experiences. Jay and the team returned home. Jay couldn't tell the story of his travel, as he knew no one would believe, but he kept on thanking god for the life-learning he had received. And this learning included the knowledge of the ill effects of the suicide, the dreaded sight that he had seen in the flood hit area, and his conversation with one of the spirits. He decided to devote his time to providing counselling to the people going through weak times and those prone to suicidal tendencies. He wanted to lend support to all those weak souls so that they could be brought back to life and not let them hang between dimensions. He was happy that he had found a purpose of his life. He also landed a very good job in the field of marine archaeology, the kind of work he always wanted to do.

And then one day, while he was on the bed, he heard someone call him.

"Jay Jay...," he could hear the voice clearly. He was trying to remember who it was.

And again, he heard, "Jay, can you hear me?"

"Professor? Is that your voice?" replied Jay, looking all around. He had recognized the voice even after a year of that incident.

"Yes, Jay. It's me."

"Where are you, Professor?"

"I am stuck in another dimension, Jay. I am reaching out for help in your dream."

And then the alarm clock buzzed, *Tring-Tring.*

It was seven in the morning. Jay realized he was in a deep sleep and was getting late for his day. He woke up, stopped the buzz, and got up for yet another day.